SHIFTER'S STORM

ICE AGE SHIFTERS BOOK 5

CAROL VAN NATTA

CHAVANCH PRESS

Shifter's Storm
(Ice Age Shifters Book 5)

Ice Age Shifters® is a registered trademark of Carol Van Natta

Cover and logo design by Amanda Kelsey of Razzle Dazzle Design

Editing by Shelley Holloway of Holloway House

Published by Chavanch Press

Copyright © 2019 by Carol Van Natta

In a dying fairy fantasyland, can two shifters tell if the magic between them is real?

While volunteering for hurricane cleanup, sheriff's deputy and leopard shifter Chantal Hammond stumbles across two escapees from a fairy fantasyland. Unfortunately, when she tries to help, she ends up trapped. She quickly discovers she's lost in a mini-world of trouble, and more captives need rescuing.

Prehistoric sloth shifter Dauro de Mar and his friends have cruelly been imprisoned in their animal forms for years. His plan to lead the escape is mostly wishful thinking until an intoxicating and magical leopard shifter arrives still in her human form. She's their game changer.

It's going to take Chantal's and Dauro's combined skills, magic, and courage to evade evil hunters and greedy fairies, and get everyone out of this mess. Especially since the fairy fantasyland is disintegrating. Can they fight off danger— and their sizzling attraction—long enough to win their freedom? Or will they be destroyed by the mother of all storms when this magical land dies?

Find out today in *Shifter's Storm*, another sizzling hot Ice Age Shifters® paranormal romance from USA TODAY bestselling author Carol Van Natta.

~ ~ ~ ~ ~

Shifter's Storm is a complete story with a happily-ever after and no cliffhanger, and can be enjoyed without having read the rest of the series.

ALSO BY CAROL VAN NATTA

Paranormal Romance

- Shifter Mate Magic (Ice Age Shifters #1)
- Shift of Destiny (Ice Age Shifters #2)
- Heart of a Dire Wolf (Ice Age Shifters #3)
- Dire Wolf Wanted (Ice Age Shifters #4)
- Shifter's Storm (Ice Age Shifters #5)
- Ice Age Shifters Collection Books 1-4

- In Graves Below (Magic, NM)

Space Opera - Central Galactic Concordance Series

- Last Ship Off Polaris-G (Novella)
- Overload Flux (Book 1)
- Minder Rising (Book 2)
- Zero Flux (Novella)
- Pico's Crush (Book 3)
- Pet Trade (Novella)
- Jumper's Hope (Book 4)
- Cats of War (Novella)
- Spark Transform (Book 5)
- Central Galactic Concordance Box Set Books 1-3

Retro Science Fiction Comedy

- Hooray for Holopticon

Dauro ya Ketumino da'Nok de Mar lumbered up onto the bank of the impossible river and snorted forcefully to open his nose and ear flaps. The pretend sun was more than halfway toward the far horizon. He shook up and down to help his fur shed water.

The world shook. Even the distant orchard trees to his left swayed.

What?

Dauro's giant aquatic sloth form was massive, but not *that* massive. Certainly not massive enough to shake an entire magical fairy demesne.

The world shook again, longer this time. Water sloshed onto the river's banks, lapping at his back paws.

When Nessireth, the ancient fairy who created the private fantasyland to house the collection of aquatic exotics she'd captured over the years, went on a rampage, the wind blew heat and the central castle trembled. But she'd died and turned to fairy dust two months ago.

A memory surfaced of feeling something similar a

couple of hundred years ago, soon after Nessireth moved the demesne from the high, cold place to a warm island location. The demesne's anchor had been tugged by a violent real-world storm she'd called a hurricane. After a second one a few years later, she'd used her then-abundant magic to add more anchors. That cured it.

Dauro also remembered a recent comment from Kelvin, the young pygmy hippopotamus shifter who had been Nessireth's final acquisition. Humans were now living *everywhere*, and they'd been burning forests and fossils. According to Kelvin, scientists said it changed the climate, and they predicted more hurricanes.

Dauro believed it. Heat and magic were similar—increased energy in a stable spell guaranteed unstable results.

More shaking. The river water surged in a wave, wetting his front paws.

Fairy demesne magic made the circular river flow constantly to provide habitat and feeding grounds for him and the other aquatic shifters and creatures. It hadn't ever changed… until today.

That brought home to him that he and others needed to get serious about escaping. Nessireth had bragged about spending millennia to construct her demesne, but it was decaying daily without her active magic to maintain it. The false moon wasn't as round as it used to be, and had a noticeable pink tint. Just last week, the constant breeze had taken to gusting chaotically.

None of the captives knew what would happen if the demesne collapsed with them still inside. Dauro was certain it wouldn't be good.

His giant sloth side liked solitary peace and quiet, but his suppressed human side knew he needed to check on the rest of his friends. Nessireth's death had given him more freedom than the others. And his limited telepathic skills as a sloth meant he had to visit them himself. Nessireth had forced each of them to remain in their animal form, and the demesne would keep them that way forever... as long as the magic held.

As the oldest of Nessireth's acquisitions, he'd become the *sinchi*, the temporary champion of the collection. In his opinion, formidable size, war experience, and a talent for magic while in animal form didn't make him a leader, but he was the best they had.

Before his energy-saving sloth succumbed to the lure of a nap, he plunged back into the water. Digging his strong, clawed toes into the silty bank, he let the water flow over him for a minute while he thought. Downstream was the long way around the river, but wouldn't tire him out as fast. So far, the magical protein-enriched sea grasses he depended on for food still grew overnight, but for how long?

He shoved off and let the current help him swim toward his friend Sunscar's territory. The closer he got, the more the magic in the water felt as agitated as the river itself.

And no wonder, because the lake's wall was breached. Instead of an orderly river running next to a placid pool, the whole area was now a flooded swamp. The demesne's castle was already repairing the wall, but the water had no natural way to drain back into the lake.

Even worse, the damage had activated the water-based defensive spells, which were fighting with the castle's defenses. Grab-weed tried to strangle the broken pieces of the wall, as if they were attackers. Two of the animated castle statues tore at the weeds so the wall could heal.

Dauro projected his thoughts as loudly as he could. *Sunscar! Are you hurt?*

After a long moment, Sunscar's answer came as clearly

as if they were in physical contact. *No need to shout. Stay away from the wall. I'll come to you.*

Dauro didn't need his friend's warning. The semi-sentient castle had strict orders to assume that interference by the captives was another escape attempt, and to react with painful consequences.

Dauro lumbered away from the churning and sat on the lawn. The water now covered his haunches.

The temperature in the demesne was never cold enough to suit him. According to old Nessireth, he was valuable because his animal side was a very rare giant throwback to the age of ice. No wonder the river always felt like being in a volcano-heated spring.

Moments later, visible arrows of surface water waves heralded the arrival of Sunscar. His giant eel form was more versatile than it looked. He could navigate through surprisingly shallow fresh or salt water by flattening into an ovoid shape and twisting like a snake.

This is a clusterfuck. Sunscar's disgruntlement came through his thoughts loud and clear.

Yes. Dauro didn't know many modern human curses, but that one had been Nessireth's last favorite. She'd learned it from one of the mercenary hunters she hired to track and capture creatures to collect or trade. *How is your farm?*

Clusterfucking earthquake tore apart my fences. My dinner is swimming free in the lake.

The demesne magically stocked and replenished all the water habitats with edible fish for Sunscar and the other piscivores. Dauro admired Sunscar's scheme to corral them so he wouldn't have to chase them around his lake when he was hungry.

I'll look for branches and help you rebuild. But we should plan on escaping soon. The demesne is falling apart.

Sunscar's tail thrashed. *You go. There's no place for me in the real world.*

Dauro-the-sloth's gusty sigh vibrated his nose flaps. *How do you know? 1879 was a long time ago. The world has changed a lot since you came here. Maybe there's a perfect place for you now.*

More tail thrashing. *Don't worry, I promise to help the rest of you escape.*

Thank you. Dauro worried about his friend but couldn't make him go if he didn't want to. *I'm checking on the others. Do you wish to come with me?*

No. I have to catch all the clusterfucking fish before sunset, or I'll starve this evening. The false moon is dark tonight.

Okay. That was Dauro's favorite word from the modern languages he'd overheard.

He raised himself up to as tall as he could stand on his hind legs to look for the faster current. The false bright sunlight of midday made him blink, as always. *I'll come back around later with wood for your pens.*

Hmph. Sunscar turned and swam away. Niceties weren't among his talents.

Dauro wished he could help with Sunscar's sadness, but he and all his friends were hanging on by threads, in one way or another. Some days, he barely remembered his own name.

Old Nessireth had known perfectly well that her collection consisted of thinking, feeling, intelligent beings. She just hadn't cared. The collection displayed her wealth and power. She relished being feared and envied by her rivals, especially the rock fairy tribe that had rejected her long ago.

Once he got back to the flowing part of the river, Dauro relaxed and let the water help him along. Sometimes, he traveled the river all day, swimming back and forth. The buoyant water helped soothe his sloth's aversion to exercise and made his human half feel like he was going somewhere.

If he was honest, he also worried about finding a place for himself in the real world. As best he could guess, he'd been in captivity for four hundred years, most of them lonely. Eagerly befriending and seeking out tales from the newer members of the collection about how civilization had grown and changed hardly prepared him to live in it.

Humans reproduced far more prolifically than magical folk, and they'd been busy. Technology gave them the edge. The hidden magical community still only agreed on one thing: Disclosing their existence to humans would be fatal. Dauro had been locked in his sloth form so long, he could barely remember walking on two legs or what it felt like to be touched on smooth skin. And the pleasures of loving were such distant memories that they felt like dreams.

The current took him around the mid-river island with a jumble of rocks that had once been a statue of Nessireth herself.

Beyond the ruined statue, away from the castle, the unfinished rainforest stood tall and unchanging, even though rain fell each afternoon. Maybe his new freedom of movement would allow him to scour it for fallen branches and to finally find out if it had a hidden door like the old rumor said.

Up ahead in the river, the castle's broad, arched bridge loomed. Both decorative and functional, it was wide enough for fifteen armored, sword-carrying human warriors to walk abreast. Except modern human warriors now carried something called assault rifles that could kill from a distance even farther than an *atlatl* sling could throw a spear. So much to learn about the real world.

Dauro slowed and projected his thoughts. *Nibi'ikwe, I give you greetings. May I come closer?*

Amusement threaded through Nibi's faint reply. *My river is your river. I promise not to drown you.*

Is the shaking bothering your home?

Nope. The river is agitated, but the bridge is steady. Do you know what's causing the turmoil?

Real-world hurricane, I think. The anchors might be failing.

Dismay colored Nibi's reply. *That's not good.*

No, agreed Dauro. He grabbed a huge gulp of air, then pushed off the bank to add to his momentum and dove downward, heading toward the huge, ornate bridge footing.

Nibi swam toward him as far as she could. A harness of magical Alfar metal around her neck and chest connected to an Alfar chain embedded in the rock of the footing.

Nibi had been caught by Nessireth's hunters in the late 1950s, a real-world time Dauro couldn't even imagine. After several nearly successful escape attempts, she'd been cruelly chained and bespelled to serve as the metaphorical troll under the bridge in the event enemies came to call. They never had, not even in the four hundred years Dauro had been captive, but fairies lived for millennia and diligently nurtured grudges.

Trolls were supposed to be ugly, but to Dauro's eyes, Nibi was stunning. She called herself a Mishipeshu, a mythical shifter from a family clan of them in the Great Lakes area of North America. Her body looked like a dark copper-colored underwater cougar with horns. Tiny scales mimicked fur, and long flat scales along her spine could rise up to make her look threatening and inedible. Her tail was long and lithe, arrow-tipped like a ray, and her paws had webbed toes with sharp claws.

Nibi's green-gold eyes glowed like gems. *Let's go up so you can breathe.*

Dauro accepted her offer with alacrity. Between the stirred-up mud and the magic, the water was prickly and uncomfortable on his eyes and nose.

He rested on the footing edge, letting the water carry his weight, with only his head above the surface.

Nibi climbed up on the ledge above the waterline. Her scales shed water quickly, making her look like an exquisite copper figure by a master artisan.

You always think the best of us. She sent an image of a Mishipeshu who had eyes of brilliant sapphire blue and whose scales glimmered like the polished gold of kings. *My sister had males of all species after her for centuries. Imagine their dismay when she life-mated with a female undine from Lake Superior.*

I like your darker color better. If Dauro were better at telepathy, he could keep his thoughts private, but he'd rather be an open book than alone.

I've been testing my limits, like you asked. I've got much more access to my water magic and I think I could shift to human, but I don't dare. The Alfar metal will burn me alive. If I'm going to escape, I still need the key. Scales rippled along her body, mirroring her agitation.

Yes, that's the thorn in the paw. Nessireth had centuries to invent spells and acquire magic charms to keep us controlled. Tomorrow, I will ask everyone to come here. We must pool our treasures and work together.

The world shook again, roiling the river. Pebbles on the shore danced with the vibration. A gust of humid wind chilled his snout.

One of Nibi's ears cocked forward. *Tell them I'll send whirlpools to fetch them if they don't come.*

Dauro snorted in amusement. *Bad idea. Young Kelvin already thinks you want to eat him.*

You're a compassionate man. Warmth accompanied the thought.

I love you all. The shaking tapered off, but he could sense the start of another tidal wave coming in the water. *We're running out of time.*

2

Sweat dripped down Deputy Sheriff Chantal Breton Hammond's neck as she eyed the fallen oak tree that blocked the muddy driveway. The size and density of the exposed roots attested to its age. Too bad hurricanes had no respect for elders.

Hurricanes were also scary. And wet. And loud, even through three pillows. She'd take a howling winter snowstorm any day.

And of course, humans just *had* to name the hurricane Chantal. She was doomed to years of teasing.

The small county and town of Barron, Florida, at the north edge of the Everglades, had escaped major damage. Maybe the elven magic spells that made humans forget the county existed worked with hurricanes, too.

She flipped opened the cover of her tablet to call up the digital map for the area. The GPS would find the address faster than she could. It was too damn hot and humid to walk up the meandering driveway to look for a house number that might not even be there.

In the Wyoming mountains, her home base when not in

the training exchange program with other law enforcement organizations, mid-September was respectably arid and cool. Certainly not pushing a hundred and one with humidity to match, with little difference at night. Sweat soaked her two braids and glued her light khaki short-sleeved uniform shirt to every inch of her skin.

"Are you lost? Let me help." Deputy Denny Fontaine, cougar shifter, strode into view from around the curve of the road. The sight of the downed tree appeared to deflate him. "Oh."

Chantal removed and replaced her tan uniform ball cap. Her inner leopard twitched its tail. She never got lost. Few shifters did, and her magic gave her an extra edge.

At forty years old, Fontaine was only ten years older than she was, but he seemed a lot younger. Considering average shifter lifespans, they were both new adults at best, but he reminded her of the sheltered pups and cubs of some overprotective families in Kotoyeesinay. Yes, she still lived with her parents, but they'd made sure she got plenty of independent experience outside the safe confines of the magical sanctuary town she'd grown up in. This was her fourth exchange assignment.

Fontaine, on the other hand, had lived in Barron all his life. Between his guaranteed job and his rent-free, double-wide bachelor pad on family property, he had every incentive to stay right where he was. His circle of friends probably wouldn't change for the next hundred years. He considered a visit to Naples, the neighboring county seat, an event. And to hear him tell it, the beach at Fort Lauderdale, eighty miles east, was a foreign country full of snotty, sneering natives.

The nature gods had done him no favors by making him the prettiest unmated male shifter around. He knew it, too. Healthy athletic build, artfully unruly blond hair, and sun-bronzed skin. Tawny-gold eyes and a winsome smile that could charm anything.

And, thank all the moon and feline goddesses of the known universe, definitely not her mate. Scent less interesting than morning cereal. No twitch on the spark gauge. Not a single thread of shifter-mate magic for miles.

Persistence, however, in spades. When she didn't immediately tumble into bed with him, he took it as a challenge. Apparently, no one had ever turned him down.

He'd tried feline-shifter moves first. Offering her the first choice of food. Draping sweaty clothes around to remind her of his scent. Crowding her space. Sniffing her neck.

When those failed, he'd gone online for "how to pick up women" groups for humans. She knew because he'd forgotten to erase the website history on the shared desktop computer in the office. Based on the techniques he'd tried, no one in those forums had ever talked to a female of *any* species.

His latest tactic seemed to involve being aggressively helpful in anything that demonstrated physical skill or handyman skills. Especially if it gave him an excuse to take off his clothes.

She had to admit he was as pretty as a billboard underwear model. However, until she'd seen Fontaine in action, she'd never run across a feline whose human side was all thumbs. No wonder none of the other deputies asked him for help. He couldn't even change a flat tire without denting the hub cap or losing the lug nuts.

As he contemplated the downed tree, his face lit up with an enthusiastic grin. "I'll get the chainsaw."

"No," said Chantal hurriedly, visions of calamity in her head. "We'd be here all day." She brandished her tablet. "Let's just tag it on the map and let the city manager's office handle it." She tilted her head toward the property. "We could see if the owner is home and needs–"

He cut her off. "Not my job."

Out of the corner of her eye, she saw his expression of frustrated discontent. He muttered something that sounded like "frigid as a frog" as he spun and marched back to the road. His hand rested on the grip of his service weapon as he walked.

She hadn't heard that barbed insult since high school. Now, it usually just made her laugh. Give her a man who'd outgrown that nonsense any day of the week.

Just as he disappeared around the curve, he yelled, "I'll be in the truck, *Probationary Junior* Deputy."

Great. He'd probably sulk the rest of the afternoon unless he got to bust heads or shoot something.

Most shifters thought guns were pointless, but the Barron cougar clan loved them. Collected them. Shot things with them—occasionally including themselves, if enough liquor was involved.

The county sheriff, Ollie Torres, ordered her to follow policy and wear a gun on duty for protection from the natural wild animals. But a handgun wouldn't stop a big predator.

Besides, it was illegal to shoot the endangered alligators, bears, and Florida panthers. And where was the fun in shooting an overpopulated deer or an exotic invasive snake when you could go four-footed to stalk and ambush it instead?

Furthermore, shifters dominated in tiny Barron County. The small, dysfunctional cougar clan had been there for centuries, hiding in the wilderness from human tribes and their wars. The larger flock of flamingo shifters came later, blown in by an early nineteenth-century hurricane. The flamingos had cleverly negotiated for the spells that made the town and county so forgettable they got left off any human records, including maps, so the cougars let them stay.

Shooting fast-healing shifters usually just made them mad. Shooting one of the ancient races was more reckless than kissing a rabid wolverine. Shooting stray tourists brought notoriety that none of magical species could afford.

And yet, the Barron cougars all just *had* to have guns. When he wasn't in cougar form, Fontaine carried three of the damn things wherever he went.

Her tablet finally signaled it had pinpointed her location, so she added a note to the coordinates about the downed tree. Barron might be an insular community trying to live down their recent disgrace, but thanks to the forward-looking flamingos, the government had state-of-the-art tech toys.

The rest of the afternoon was as hot and annoying as she'd predicted. When Fontaine tried to pick a fight, she kept her cool and laughed it off, but just barely.

The Sheriff's Station owed its welcome cooler air to the city building's new air-conditioning system, powered by rooftop solar panels and experimental, magically enhanced batteries.

At her shared desk, she connected the tablet to the tower computer and copied all the reports to the local network. The files should already be synced to the cloud, but redundant copies never hurt.

"Hey, Hammond." Torres's bass voice came from his office.

As usual, Fontaine had disappeared two seconds after their shift ended, leaving her to do the hand-off to Osborne, the cougar male on evening patrol.

The dispatchers and the other deputies were cougar males, too. She was the first female they'd had in the department in decades. Maybe ever. They'd had to trade with a fairy shop up north to tailor the uniform shirts and brown tactical pants to fit her. She was lucky they'd given her a nameplate and an ID badge.

In her first month, she'd done ride-alongs with all the cougars at one time or another. But even after three months, she still wasn't yet cleared to work any shift by herself, not even dispatch. It rubbed her fur the wrong way, but she doubted they'd loosen the leash for the last month of her assignment.

At least they didn't seem resentful toward her as a confident female, like she'd seen in some ultra-conservative canine packs. It helped that her outsized black leopard could hold her own with any of their cougars.

It also helped that she'd proven she had a lot of free magic and knew how to use it. The newbie hazing had stopped quickly after her spell caused anyone who touched her gear without permission to experience a long and violent sneeze attack.

She stood and crossed to the sheriff's open door. "Yes, sir?"

"Two things. One, starting tomorrow, you'll be riding with Osborne for the next four... Where's your weapon?" His left eye twitched as he glared at the gap on her utility belt where her holster should be.

Chantal tilted her head toward the storage room. "Locked up in the gun safe."

He was smart enough not to yell at her about following the official end-of-shift regulation he chose to let the others ignore, but his narrowed eyes said he didn't like it.

She tilted her head toward the whiteboard on his wall with shift notations. "Osborne's vacation starts the day after tomorrow. I can take his last night shift–"

"No," he interrupted, "you don't know when to let

things… you don't know the county well enough. Shit. I'll set the rest of your schedule tomorrow."

It took conscious effort to keep her expression neutral. She'd jailed his hard-drinking, mate-terrorizing cousin Verna a couple of weeks ago. He likely knew she'd do it again, too. That cougar was a menace. "You said two things?"

A sour look settled on his face. "Oh, that. Mayor Belinda wants to see you in her office about some volunteer 'opportunity.'" A curled lip conveyed his scorn. "Her flock controls our budget, so be polite when you shut her down."

"Of course." She spun away quickly, before he noticed she wasn't on board with his attitude.

Torres wasn't a bad man, but he needed to find a job he actually liked. One where he could discipline employees or arrest miscreants without getting in trouble with clan or family.

Admittedly, she'd been spoiled. She'd grown up admiring the world's best sheriff. He was the reason she'd joined law enforcement. She missed Tanner, Shiloh, and all her colleagues in Kotoyeesinay. They were her friends as well as her coworkers. Emails and video chats didn't make up for seeing and smelling them. Or playing elaborate practical jokes on Tanner, or racing cheetah-shifter I'itame around the block, or planning a surprise anniversary party for Shiloh and his husband.

As far as she could tell, Torres's major flaw was blind loyalty to his cougar-shifter clan. On top of that, he shared a tangled family tree with most of them. The Shifter Tribunal had believed his insistence that he had no idea his clan had been robbing the town blind for decades and killing to hide it.

The Tribunal, with its flexible view of ethics, would have probably left the cougars alone, except their last murder was a big-city investigative journalist. The Tribunal only barely managed to cover up the crime as a hunting accident to derail the Florida Department of Law Enforcement's investigation and keep the feds out of it.

The daylighted corruption was the town's big, shameful secret that no one talked about. She'd only found out because her mother had friends who worked at the Tribunal. Torres had barely kept his sheriff job when the town and county governments fell apart.

He certainly deeply resented the flamingos. They'd swept the slate of special elections after a dozen guilty cougars got hauled off to shifter jail. The convicted cougars would stay there for a few decades, until the humans forgot about them. In the meantime, the leadership vacuum left the town and county administration in shambles. Flamingos picked up the pieces.

In Barron, no one cared about the color of a shifter's skin or the pattern of fur or feathers, or paid attention to human political tempests, but they sure got exercised over clans.

Based on the cold shoulder she'd received from the cougars, even if she stayed for forty years instead of four months, she'd always be the outsider. The flamingo colony took togetherness and group activities too far for her comfort, but they'd at least invited her to their picnics and parties.

She texted the affable Deputy Osborne that she'd brief him after she got back from the meeting. Some information didn't belong in official daily activity reports.

Her shirt had dried in the air-conditioned office, but her braids were stiff with sweat and she still smelled like a steam room. Nothing she could do about it. Besides, shifter senses meant they all knew exactly what—and who—the other shifters had been doing. Which was another reason

Fontaine hadn't attracted her. He clearly liked plenty of variety in his bed. To her, sex without the emotional connection was less interesting than an afternoon nap in a high tree.

A mate would be fascinating. She rolled her eyes. Her inner leopard had a one-track mind.

She slid the tablet into the desk drawer designated as hers, then cast a tiny security spell to lock the tablet's cover until she released it. Not that she was fluff-headed enough to use department equipment for personal messages, like a certain blond cougar deputy.

The Sheriff's Station was at one end of the L-shaped county building. She walked past the county offices at the center to the other end that housed the smaller town staff. Everyone tended to keep earlier business hours in the summer to avoid the oppressive heat, but from what she'd seen, Mayor Belinda worked overtime more days than not.

Chantal politely knocked on the pebbled-glass door, then opened it and went in.

Belinda looked up from an open laptop on her desk. "Deputy Hammond, what a nice surprise." Her exaggerated Southern accent made Chantal chuckle. She was a short, rounded woman with light brown skin and laughing eyes. Her intensely orange-pink linen pantsuit mimicked the color of her flamingo form.

"You wanted to see me?"

Belinda clicked her mouse twice, then closed the laptop. "That Fontaine cub gone already, is he?" Subtle disapproval laced her tone.

"I think Deputy Fontaine is around somewhere." Chantal wasn't one to give up her coworkers, even when they irritated her. "Did you want to talk to him, too?"

"No, thank you." She waved to a chair as she picked up her phone to send a text. "I'm asking Renée to join us."

Chantal sat. Recently elected county commissioner Renée Reyes was another flamingo shifter. Probably older than Belinda, but it was hard to tell with shifters, and it wasn't always polite to ask. Renée also happened to be true-mated to a cougar shifter who worked for the much larger neighboring county's Sheriff's Department. Chantal imagined that had been the scandal of its day.

She didn't mind waiting. Nothing on her agenda for the evening. No place to go, either, since sleepy Barron couldn't hold a candle to her last assignment in New Orleans.

Besides, her jumbled work schedule made social plans impossible. After a shower and a meal at the all-hours diner, she might go furry for a midnight skulk through the stand of tall cypress trees a dozen miles north. She liked them better than the messy palm trees that residents planted just because everyone else did.

Unlike her other exchange assignments, she hadn't made any new friends in Barron. Guilt poked at her for not trying harder, since making connections with people outside her hometown was supposed to be one of the features of the program.

Her inner leopard wanted to meet more people, too, if it meant finding her mate. Chantal liked the idea, too… in theory. Her shaggy-prehistoric-bear, true-mated parents had a fantastic relationship, and she wanted one just like it. Trouble was, she was only her mother's biological daughter.

The less said about her leopard-shifter sperm-donor father and his family, the better. She worried she might have inherited their tendency to cat around, so she was extra choosy. She could count the number of lovers she'd had on one hand and still have fingers left over. Despite her inner leopard's growing impatience to be mated, very long shifter lives meant she didn't have to figure it out this decade.

It would be good to have someone warm to nap with. Her leopard pictured a large, soft bed next to a fireplace in a cozy winter cabin. Chantal couldn't argue with that. But she wanted a lover who would be there when she woke up, too.

The mayor's well-padded visitor chair was more comfortable than the creaky metal monstrosity at her temporary desk. She melted into it.

The mayoral office was suitably large and styled to look prestigious without being tacky. From scent traces, a long-gone previous occupant had smoked a lot of Cuban cigars, and someone had recently eaten a shrimp salad for lunch. The air vents were much quieter. Maybe after tomorrow's night shift, she'd try tightening the vent covers in the Sheriff's Station. The one near her desk sounded like a kazoo when the fans kicked in.

Renée arrived moments later, carrying a tablet. She was blonde, blue-eyed, and lived in khakis and sleeveless blouses. Chantal didn't know how she stayed looking so neat and elegant, considering she was the county's social worker with a passel of her own cubs plus some foster fledglings as well.

After the obligatory offer of refreshments, Belinda got straight to the point.

"Renée and I are part of an international charity that does relief work in southern Florida and around the Caribbean. We're organizing a trip to Vieques, a small island off Puerto Rico, to help with recovery efforts."

Renée nodded earnestly. "Actually, our Puerto Rican relatives are doing the organizing, we're just recruiting." She opened her tablet and brought up a gallery of photos. "Your namesake hurricane did serious damage to the whole island." The enlarged pictures showed debris everywhere. Flattened trees, boats in pieces, houses with no roofs. "Rain washed out the roads and trails, too." More pictures showed significant flood damage. "The military's former bomb practice was bad enough, but this hit *everything*.

Belinda waved toward the tablet. "After the last direct-hit hurricane, the human government ignored Puerto Rico and Vieques for years. We're not going to let that happen this time. Our *friends* live there."

As near as Chantal could tell, Florida flamingo shifters were either related to or allied with every other flamingo-shifter flock and colony in the Western Hemisphere. They blended in with the natural wild flocks and cared for them. They'd even herded them south, away from Florida, once humans started hunting them for their pink feathers to decorate hats.

"We'd like to know," said Renée, "if you'd be interested in volunteering for a couple of weeks."

Chantal blinked, surprised. "You mean go to Vieques? I'm flattered, but I'm trained as a first responder, not in recovery work. And I'd be leaving the Sheriff's Department short-handed."

"Yes, but you speak Spanish and you're self-reliant." Renée smiled and waggled a finger between herself and Belinda. "We flamingos can't decide what to have for breakfast without a community forum and runoff votes."

"It's true," Belinda agreed with a chuckle. "Half of Vieques is a protected wilderness. Your mountain-rescue experience and your feline abilities are just what are needed to assess the damage and help prioritize rehabilitation projects. From what we've seen, you know when to take initiative and when to call for help."

Chantal had to admit the opportunity was tempting. Her inner leopard loved independent exploring and discovering things. Keeping the peace in Barron consisted mostly of issuing tickets for expired license plates, serving warrants, and keeping drunk-ass shifters from tearing up the local taverns and shooting each other. Luckily, sensitive shifter noses detested the smells of drug cooking, or the county might have had a more serious problem.

On the other hand, she took her job seriously. "It's not fair to leave the department down one deputy."

Belinda exchanged a look with Renée, then turned to Chantal. "You wouldn't be. We enticed Sheriff Torres into joining the Tribunal's law enforcement exchange program by promising to fund the new position outside the department's budget. We thought it would be a good way to introduce new ideas." She made a frustrated hiss. "Instead, he's found every excuse to delay sending one of his deputies away. They're at full staff without you. We recently found out he's given you a deliberately random schedule and crappy assignments so you'll quit. That way, he can call the program a failure."

Realization blossomed in Chantal as facts took on a new light. "Well, that certainly explains a lot." She shook her head. "I just thought they were in disarray after the town, er, unincorporated."

Renée hooted with laughter. "That's how the cougars are describing it now?"

Chantal snorted. "They don't talk about it at all. I only know what you told me on the first day and what I overhear in the diner."

"The cougars stole so much the town went bankrupt," said Belinda. "Or would have, if our flock hadn't stepped in. Our loan kept us off the state treasurer's radar and out of the state courts."

"Oh, I see." Chantal nodded, putting more pieces together. "You let Torres stay because he's a Barron cougar, not necessarily because he's the best person for the job."

Belinda and Renée exchanged another look.

Renée sighed. "Yeah, that about sums it up. Not all the

cougars were corrupt. Some had no clue and some were horrified, and that includes Torres. They should have some representation in the government." She shook her head. "To be fair, being sheriff is a stressful job that no one else wants. Torres commands respect from his cougar clan where they wouldn't listen to a flamingo or anyone else."

Belinda waggled her eyebrows suggestively. "So, are you interested in getting filthy hot and sweaty for two weeks?"

Renée smirked.

Chantal laughed. "And that's different from Barron in what way? Yeah, I'm interested. It seems fitting, since my namesake storm caused the damage. How do I get there—fairy portal?"

"No. Very strange," said Renée. "Fairy portals can't open anywhere near Vieques. Witch and wizard portals can't, either. We'll get you ported to Puerto Rico and arrange a boat to take you to the island. The flamingos on the team will probably shift and fly." A corner of her mouth quirked. "Heavy boats make us seasick."

"That'll work." Chantal resolved to study a map when she got to her computer in her rented mobile home. It was too embarrassing to admit she only had a vague impression that Puerto Rico was south of Florida somewhere in the Caribbean, and she'd never heard of the island.

Belinda opened her laptop again. "It'll have to be unpaid leave from the department, but the flock will make up your salary."

Chantal shook her head. "Donate it to the cause. Just supply the equipment I'll need and feed me, and we'll call it even. When do you want me to leave?"

"As soon as possible." Renée brought up a calendar on her tablet. "Could you go tomorrow night at eight? They've already reserved a supply boat."

No wonder they'd won their elections. Flamingos liked

organizing things, but these two were the queens of efficiency. "Sure, if I can get some things from home. Boots that fit. Wilderness gear. Clean underwear."

Belinda beamed. "You phone home, and I'll break the news to Torres and get the Pink Ladies to arrange the portal." She started typing on her computer.

"The Pink Ladies? Is that a tribe of fairies?" asked Chantal.

Renée laughed. "It's the charity. The real name is Las Damas Rosadas del Paraiso. The 'Rose Women of Paradise' sounds like a brothel to American ears, so we just say 'Pink Ladies.'" Her fingers worked rapidly on her tablet.

Belinda looked up. "Let's not keep you here any longer. We'll keep you posted by text. Send us a list of anything you want added to that supply boat."

Chantal knew a polite dismissal when she heard one. She stood.

Renée put down her tablet and stood as well. "We really appreciate your willingness to do this, especially on such short notice."

To Chantal's surprise, Renée enveloped her in a warm, strong hug.

Chantal shrugged, a bit embarrassed. "I like looking out for people."

"You're a good person. We owe you for putting up with the sheriff's bad behavior and our neglect," said Belinda. "Go get some sleep. You'll probably need it."

3

"You! Big fat mammal with pointy snout and claws! Come here!"

The shouted words came from the taller of the two rock fairies who stood on the high, flat boulder that had once served as part of a dock. Behind them, the walkway curved from the castle's back doors to Dauro's home habitat area.

A push of geas magic from a blue wand accompanied the order, compelling him to obey. It wasn't the demesne's geas, so he could have resisted, but he was curious.

Hours before, the pair had dropped from the unreal sky and landed with a tremendous thump on the back lawn, close to his lair. They'd obviously breached the demesne's portal.

By the time Dauro had swum closer, the four nearest castle statues had already come to life and were marching toward the interlopers.

The fairies waved charms and spoke words he didn't understand. Magic buffeted his senses like a howling wind and rippled throughout the demesne. The castle statues stopped their advance, then returned to their pedestals and plinths. The castle's gigantic back doors, which had been closed for decades, creaked open to full width. The fairies marched in like they owned the place.

Apparently, they did.

"Out of the water!" yelled the shorter fairy. She held a large, open book in her hands. "We know you can understand us. Nessie's book says so."

"Don't make us get nasty!" shouted the taller fairy, waving the wand. Another punch of magic pushed at him.

The taller, wand-waving fairy had short and curly, pale-blue hair with pink striations, blue-gray skin, and blue-and-orange speckled eyes. The shorter fairy had straight and long quartz-white hair, blue skin with pink marbling, and sky-blue eyes.

Like old Nessireth, they had sharp, pointy teeth and sharp claws on their fingers and toes. Unlike Nessireth, they wore clothing. The taller fairy pulled at the cloth on her legs as if it scratched. She carried an ornately carved stone box.

Dauro pulled himself up out of the river and sat on the sandy bank. He'd already asked Sunscar, with his superior telepathic skill, to alert everyone in the demesne of the new arrivals. They all planned to lie low and play as dumb as dirt.

The shorter fairy with the book pointed to herself. "I am Trixis and this"—she pointed to her taller companion—"is Omorachi. We are the heirs and new owners of the demesne and everything in it, now that our horrible harridan aunt is finally dead."

"About effin' time, too," muttered the taller fairy.

The shorter fairy looked down at the book, then up again. "You're supposed to be a shifter, so shift."

Dauro tilted his head quizzically. From his height advantage, he could see the open pages had detailed sketches of him as a sloth and a lot of cramped, uneven rows of symbols. He finally recognized the tome as Nessireth's precious record book.

Trixis peered closer at the pages, squinting. "I wish we could figure out what his name is. This is the worst script I've ever seen."

"Let's try a shortcut." Omorachi opened the stone box. "Which is the alpha charm?"

Trixis flipped to another section of the book. "The bone."

Omorachi lifted a heart-shaped avian bone and pointed it at Dauro. "I order you to shift."

A flavor of magic Dauro hadn't felt in centuries buffeted him, but rolled on by with no effect. He was immune to alpha commands from any species of shifter he'd ever met. Always had been, much to the annoyance of the various insecure alphas who'd tried to dominate him.

Besides, even if the charm had worked, the demesne's much stronger controlling magic would have forced him to shift back almost immediately. When she first bought him, Nessireth had done it five times in rapid succession to prove it, and as a demonstration of her punishment methods. Not even raptors shifted that fast in the real world. His bones had ached for days, despite speedy shifter healing.

Omorachi waved the bone again. "Change! Shift!"

The magic rolled on by. Interesting that alpha power could be captured in a charm and wielded by a non-shifter.

"Here, let me try." Trixis snatched the charm away from Omorachi and ordered Dauro to shift.

The magic had no effect. He yawned. The heat of the day was making him sleepy. His human side prodded him to stay vigilant and learn.

"See?" Omorachi sneered. "I told you Nessie mixed rubbish in with the good stuff to fool thieves." She tilted her chin toward the charm. "That's likely the wishbone from a turkey feast."

Trixis sniffed it and made a face. "Too bad she didn't choke on it." She threw it into the water.

Dauro memorized the location. In that part of the river, the currents eddied, meaning he might be able to find the charm again and add it to his hoard of discarded treasures.

A gust of wind ruffled Dauro's fur and stirred the grass. Omorachi wrinkled her nose. "I don't remember this place stinking so bad when we came here as younglings. We're going to need a fumigator or no one will want to come." She pointed toward the book. "Turn back to the page with the list of charms. Maybe something else in this stupid box will work."

"I am not your servant." Trixis slammed the book shut. "Just take shots of him as he is. We can get his other form later."

Blowing out a whistling sigh, Omorachi shoved her box into Trixis's arms, then pulled a flat rectangle out of a small glittery pouch that was strapped around her waist.

She pressed the narrow edge, then dragged her finger over one flat side, as if drawing a magical symbol. After a few more taps, she held up the rectangle. "Us first!"

Trixis leaned close to Omorachi. They both froze and bared their teeth in what could have been a smile or a threat display. It was hard to tell with rock fairies. After the rectangle made a faint clicking sound, they relaxed.

Omorachi held up the rectangle between her and Dauro. "Show us your good side, baby!"

A tiny light flashed, but he couldn't feel any magic. Maybe it was what young Kelvin called technology.

After two more flashes, Omorachi slid the device back in her pouch. "Mammal, clean up this mess." She waved toward the jumble of lawn furniture left by the flood.

"Nessie's book says you're supposed to maintain something, so hop to it. But don't go anywhere. We'll want to talk to you later."

They both giggled and started back up the walkway toward the castle.

Omorachi pointed toward the book. "Let's go find the *draco aqua* shifter next. The book says they can talk while still an animal. We'll order her to tell us about the others."

Trixis shoved the box back into Omorachi's arms. "No, I'm thirsty, and this book is heavy. Nessie used to brag about her fairy dew collection and never even shared a thimbleful. Just 'cause the tribe laughed at her and her freaky-ass collections. I want some liquid fortification before I go traipsing around this stinky demesne a minute longer. Smells like a zoo." She detoured to wipe her bare feet on the grass, leaving furrows in the sod with her claws.

"Fine," said Omorachi in a long-suffering whiny tone. "We'll look for the sodding key to the cellar. But we need gobs of pics for the broker, or no one will nibble."

Dauro stayed on the bank, listening but not understanding half their words, until they disappeared into the castle. Testing the air with his nose, he didn't notice anything particularly pungent. The demesne hardly smelled of anything. Maybe four hundred years had killed his sense of smell.

He slid into the water, downstream of where the alpha charm went in, then walked sloth-slow upstream to where the whirling currents played.

The shifter gods must have been in a momentary good mood, because the bone was caught on some exposed roots. It was well worth the mouthful of sticks and silt to rescue it. He dove deep to his underwater stash, opening his lips to let the water help wash the dirt off his tongue.

The charm was so tiny, he was afraid of crushing or

losing it with his big claws, so he twisted his head up and into the small, grass-lined chamber and let it drop from his teeth. He used his magic and his long, dexterous tongue to secure it in the reeds.

That done, he concentrated his thoughts on his friend. *Sunscar, we all must gather now.*

Yes. We're already at Nibi's bridge. Come as fast as you can. I'll have to sift your memories of what happened. I can't read the new fairies' thoughts any better than I could read Nessireth's.

Dauro pushed into the center where the fastest river current ran and folded his front paws up under him to offer the least resistance while he kicked with his back legs.

Several minutes later, he grabbed a big lungful of air, then dove for Nibi's lair.

The sight of them all was startling. He'd never seen the entire collection gathered before. Nessireth hadn't ever let them do that. His inner human gave them a big, beaming smile for how beautiful they all were and how much he loved them.

We think the world of you, too. Nibi's warm thoughts mixed with her amusement.

Sorry. He shared his embarrassment. *I'll try to contain my thoughts.*

No need, replied Yipkash, one of the two mythological capricorn shifters that Nessireth had added to the collection about fifteen years before. She was true-mated to the other goat-with-fish-tail, Rayapkhal, who hovered protectively. Their intricately woven shifter-mate bond glowed even in the shadowed underwater depths. *You wouldn't be you if you didn't share.*

Kelvin, the young pygmy hippopotamus shifter, swam closer. Or perhaps more accurately, put Dauro between himself and Sunscar and Nibi, who both scared the daylights out of him. Dauro felt guilty for not spending more time helping Kelvin get past his animal's survival instincts and make friends with them.

Rosinette floated nearby, green blood leaking from her crippled sea wyvern wings. Old Nessireth, rightly wary of tremendously powerful wyvern magic, had cruelly pierced the wings with Alfar metal rods held tightly together with a locked chain. The shackles not only prevented flight, but were bespelled to prevent Rosinette from being able to speak in her shifted form the way other wyverns could. Despite all that and what had to be constant pain, she had a surprisingly sunny outlook.

Plunging his rear claws into the bank to stabilize his position, Dauro focused his thoughts. *I assume Sunscar relayed what the fairies said and did. We must escape before they can do whatever they have planned.*

They're going to sell us, declared Kelvin angrily. *They took your picture with a cell phone so they can put it online.*

Dauro understood the first part, but the last was meaningless. What they didn't know could get them killed.

Sunscar's mottled fins fluttered in agitation. After a stretch of silence, he calmed. *I promised Dauro I'd help with the escape. If I shift to my wraith form, I can transfer some of Kelvin's modern knowledge to all of you. You'll feel terror like you've never known, and you might have a headache for hours. But you won't be crippled by ignorance.*

Kelvin's legs churned, sending him to the surface.

Not if it will hurt Kelvin, declared Yipkash. She brushed her tail against Kelvin's flank in reassurance as he gulped air.

Sunscar darted away, then back. *He's the only one who it won't hurt. I can't do anything about the fear—it's what wraiths do. My magic started working again after Nessireth died.*

Will it hurt you? asked Dauro. Sunscar's grumpy demeanor hid a softer heart.

No, replied Sunscar. *I eat fear.*

From that, Dauro assumed Sunscar's wraith form fed on fear the way his eel form fed on fish.

Yipkash swam to the surface for a private conversation with Kelvin. Dauro envied her skill at that. In sloth form, he was either sending thoughts to no one or everyone. His human side had better control.

After long moments, both Yipkash and Kelvin swam down again.

Okay, I'll do it. Kelvin's telepathic voice felt scared but determined.

I will be first, said Dauro, touched by Kelvin's stalwart courage. *The others can decide after they see what happens to me.*

You're braver than I am, thought Nibi. Her thoughts pictured a trembling copper-colored cougar trapped in a hunter's cage.

I'm not braver. Just... more experienced with being afraid. I was a warrior for a hundred years before I ended up here.

I need air as a wraith. Sunscar darted upward.

Dauro followed. He needed air, too.

As he breached the surface, Sunscar's form morphed into the shape of a black-skinned human man. Dauro had always heard that wraiths were ghosts, but Sunscar looked decidedly solid and muscular. Scars and intricate runes decorated his chest, arms, and legs. Long coils of silver hair trailed down his back, twining like snakes in a basket. He hung in the air, his toes a paw's width above the water.

The moment after Dauro took a breath, Sunscar's hypnotic, red-eyed gaze caught his, and the fear began.

Memories of every horrific thing he'd ever seen or felt swirled in his head.

Pain rose, too, like an iron vice on his temples. Like the one used by the vengeful Spanish conquistador sorcerer who enjoyed torturing native prisoners of war to death. Then he'd discovered shifters felt just as much pain but were harder to kill. Dauro savored the justice of introducing the conquistador to a giant sloth with three angry claws that sliced through the shiny armor into the soft belly underneath.

Fear surged again, but he rode it out by remembering other triumphs in countless skirmishes.

Pain and pressure increased, but with them came a flood of images that distracted him from everything else. Birds of metal... no, jets. Fast cars. Music from boxes. Computers. Guns. Game consoles. Television. Water beds. Wars. The internet. Moon flight. A colosseum filled with more people than he'd ever seen at once. Basketball. Sweet flakes of food in colorful boxes. Buildings that touched the sky. Smart phones. Selfies.

The fear cut off. Sunscar lowered into the water, shimmering into his eel form.

Dauro barely remembered to suck in a big gulp of air before sinking back down. Shaking his head didn't help bring order to the tumble of memories that crowded his mind.

Ideally, you should take a long nap, said Sunscar. *Helps with the pain and blending the concepts. Words will come more slowly because I gave you a new language. You might have a few memories that aren't your own, but they'll fade with time.*

Dauro? asked Nibi, concern in her thoughts.

I will live, replied Dauro. *The headache is bad, but it's worth it. The real world will be a wondrous place.*

It won't hurt as much for the rest of you, said Sunscar. *Dauro's the oldest. He had more catching up to do, and didn't speak English.*

We refuse, thought Rayapkhal forcefully. *We are leaving at once.*

The others turned to the capricorns in surprise.

Rayapkhal, chided Yipkash. *Tell them why.*

A mass of bubbles exploded from her mate. *With the return of our magic, we found a way out. We can feel every drop of moisture in the demesne. It's leaking near one of the anchors. We can become one with the water for short periods. None of you can.* Rayapkhal's tone was ogre-angry, but Dauro sensed worry and fear underneath.

Yipkash sent wordless apologies. *Please forgive him. We are pregnant. We had long thought our union to be barren, but after Nessireth's demise, we both now carry fertilized eggs. If we don't get to the sacred sea, they will be born as fish to be eaten by Sunscar.*

Sunscar swam in a small circle, mouth gaping in deep offense. *I would never eat your offspring!*

I didn't mean it that way, soothed Yipkash. *I meant that without our full magic and the bower of the Icarian Sea, they'd be no more sentient than the food fish the demesne makes for you and Nibi. It is our blessing and our curse.*

Quiet Rosinette shared her thoughts. *Then you must go. I will help you all I can, after Sunscar cures my ignorance.*

The chorus of agreement pounded in Dauro's aching head.

Yes, you must go, Dauro agreed. *I will help, too. Now is the time, before the fairies figure out how to renew the demesne's control magic.*

There was no hiding an animal Dauro's size, so his and Kelvin's part in the hastily planned escape was to make a distracting ruckus at the other end of the demesne. Nibi would churn the waters, Rosinette would use her awakening magic to hide the capricorns, and Sunscar would keep in mental contact with them all and warn them if the castle defenses woke.

Dauro's head still hurt, but spending time with Kelvin was helping integrate the new knowledge. *Tell me who the laughing brown-skinned woman is in your thoughts. She wears pale green and has tightly braided hair with beads.*

Kelvin paddled in the river water behind Dauro. The pretend sun was a streak of light at the fake horizon that would soon be gone. Thirty minutes later, a fat sliver of the false moon would rise.

My aunt. She's a surgical nurse. We were going to San Francisco to visit my grandparents from Liberia. Hunters tricked us. Took us right out of the airport. She fought back hard, almost got away, but they shot her twice with a dart gun, then me. We woke up in an auction house. They sold shifters like slaves. His anger and hurt were palpable. *Nessireth told me not to get comfortable. She bought me to trade for something else she really wanted.*

New associations fluttered into Dauro's head. Humans had captured and sold Kelvin's ancestors the same way the conquistadors had enslaved the indigenous peoples of South America, where Dauro had grown up. The Spanish also brought dark-skinned slaves with them, but many escaped. His magic-wielding mother had been one of them.

A world map was now part of his understanding. Humans of all races had only finally outlawed the appalling practice a century ago. The pernicious legacy lingered in separation, prejudice, and opportunities denied. He wished he could say magical species were better, but there they both were, shiny collector's items in a dying fairy demesne.

Dauro sought for something to take Kelvin's attention. *Are you black like Sunscar when you're human?*

No, brown, like my aunt. He sent an image of himself in a

photo, with close-braided hair and a grin as wide as his cheekbones. *What do you look like?*

I am not sure anymore. He buried his fear that he'd be stuck in sloth form forever, even if they won their freedom. Kelvin and the others needed him to be strong, so that's what he'd be. *Let's go to the island with the stones. Those don't belong to the castle.*

Dauro angled toward the shallows and climbed up onto the shore. Kelvin scrambled nimbly behind him and up onto the dry sand. *I've never been here before. What are all these things?*

Nessireth said it was a statue of her. She got drunk on dew one night and told me she'd kept it to remind her of her treacherous family. If Trixis and Omorachi are her relatives, I can understand the feeling.

Kelvin ducked his head near what looked like part of a giant carved foot with curving claws. *My human friend Pete got put in foster care 'cause his real family was into gangs and drugs.*

Sometimes, it's best. I didn't fit in with—

Ready, said Sunscar in their minds. *Yipkash and Rayapkhal are at their spot. Rosinette and Nibi are ready. Start the noise.*

Dauro snorted to open his nose, then began a low and rising bellow.

Kelvin squealed a warbling call, bobbing his head up and down.

After checking to make sure the castle statues were ignoring him and Kelvin, Dauro bellowed again, higher and louder this time.

He was just warming up. In his youth, he'd discovered he could be heard for several valleys around if he put his mind to it. It felt good to call. To his sloth, it was singing.

Turning toward the castle, he let loose with another bellow. The sound echoed off the hard stone and faded.

It was probably too much to hope that they were disturbing the fairies already, but the night was young.

Climbing higher on a larger, flat piece of stone gave Kelvin a better spot from which to squeal shorter bursts. *I'm a wolf, howling at the moon!*

Amusement added an uneven wobble to Dauro's answering bellow. *You're prettier than a wolf.*

Kelvin bobbed his head. *I smell better, too.*

Dauro snorted with laughter. *Who doesn't?*

Sunscar's strong thoughts interrupted. *Keep up the noise! The capricorns are almost free!*

Kelvin squealed more wolf calls. *A-roooo! This is my pack! This is my mountain!*

Taking deep breaths, Dauro let loose with a series of long, loud bellows that vibrated his whole body. Singing of their desperate need. Of the mind-numbing loneliness that ate at his sanity. Calling for the mate he'd never had and likely never would. Who'd want to tie herself to an Ice Age behemoth?

He imagined sending his song beyond the confines of the demesne, letting the real world know they were there.

He'd always wished for someone to answer, but in four hundred long years, no one ever had.

4

Chantal would have missed the truck altogether if a momentary gleam hadn't caught her eye.

Crouching, she borrowed her leopard's senses. Yes, there it was, up the ravine, smelling of oil and gasoline.

A produce truck that big should have been easy to spot by flying flamingo shifters, but the low foliage and flood-driven debris on top camouflaged it well.

The island of Vieques was like the photos Renée and Belinda had shown her, and yet so much more.

And after Hurricane Chantal finished scouring it, so much less.

Human-built structures fared badly. Taller trees had been uprooted or broken into matchsticks. The short, squat trees had done better. Native plants and wildlife looked battered, but stubbornly clung to life.

Even though she wasn't thirsty yet, she took a small sip from her flexible, charmed canteen, then put it back on her belt. Dehydration could be even sneakier than a sly black leopard.

Regular radio was iffy on the part of the island near the

wildlife refuge. Luckily, she had something better. She keyed it on.

"Kitty One to Base."

After a moment, Leticia's Spanish-accented voice responded. *"Base to Kitty One. Please thank your Shifter Tribunal friend again for the magical satellite radio sets. However, the GPS tracker says you're in the ocean, halfway to Puerto Rico. Any dolphin or dragon ancestors you wish to tell us about?"*

Chantal laughed. "No, I'm on the wilderness road about three miles... uh, five kilometers from where Road 200 turns northeast. I found the truck."

"Isn't Elisa with you?"

"No, she didn't feel well, and no one else was awake. Before it got too hot, I figured I'd take a quick hike to where Señor Santiago thought the driver might have left it."

"Híjola... I'll talk to her."

"No, don't. She means well, but her flamingo thinks my leopard wants her for dinner, and not the kind with tablecloths and menus."

Even after three days of working together, very few of the volunteer or native flamingo shifters could stay around Chantal for very long, even though there were twenty of them to her one. Back in Barron, Belinda and Renée had gotten so comfortable being around predatory felines that they'd forgotten that most flamingos weren't.

Very little fazed Leticia, however, which was likely why she was running the whole volunteer operation and interacting with the locals. *"Okay, sorry. We'll try to do better."* After a moment, she swore. *"Now the GPS says you're in the Virgin Islands. Can you mark where you are so we can find it again?"*

Thanks to her magic, Chantal could get back there with no trouble, but that wouldn't help anyone else. "Yeah, I'll think of something. But I smell gasoline. Before I come back, I want to make sure it's not going to set the wilderness refuge on fire."

"That would be very bad. I know you're level-headed, but be careful. Call within the hour, or I'm sending rescuers after you."

"Yes, ma'am. Talk to you again soon."

Chantal keyed the radio off and snugged it back into the holster she wore on her belt.

With no humans around to see or flamingos to terrify, she shifted to her leopard form. She'd worked diligently to learn the tricks of fast shifts and using her free magic during her shift so she didn't have to shed her clothes and gear first. They came naturally to her Ice Age bear-shifter family and other Ice Age shifters she knew, but she was just a plain black leopard with a hodge-podge of free magic. Those skills had taken her a lot longer to master.

Seconds later, she was padding carefully through the ragged undergrowth. The rush of feline sensory input told her about the woodpecker tapping for insects somewhere over the ridge, the pounceable lizard scuttling through the undergrowth, and the nose-wrinkling scent of gasoline pervading the air. Almost worse than randy cougar piss.

She gave a sprawling cactus wide berth, which put her on the upslope side of the ravine, looking down into the truck. It looked undamaged, but mired in drying mud and covered with tree debris.

One paw at a time, she crept closer, checking for unstable ground and hidden hazards. Moments later, she jumped onto the cab's roof and crouched. A quick look inside confirmed the driver's story that he'd left the keys in the ignition.

Countless trips with her independent trucker dad and six years in the Sheriff's Department had made her give up any pretense of understanding why people did the things they did. Like driving on a rutted dirt road during a damn hurricane, then abandoning the truck to *walk* home in that same hurricane.

She'd like to figure out how to get the truck back onto the road. The people on the island had a hard enough life as it was without losing a valuable vehicle.

The gasoline smell came from a rusted and dented green jerry can. It hung upside down, trapped by branches, slowly leaking from its closed pour spout into a growing pool on the truck bed. She caught the branch in her claws and shook the can loose. It clattered onto its side on the bed next to the wooden rail.

A faraway faint dripping sound teased her leopard's ears and curiosity. This part of the island got very little moisture, torrential storms notwithstanding. The dripping seemed to come from up and over the hill to the east.

She turned away and jumped from the truck's roof back onto the sloping ravine, resolutely padding toward the road. Cats thought they were invincible solitary explorers, but humans knew that unfamiliar wilderness could be unforgiving.

Just as she reached the level ground of the graded road, another noise caught her attention. It sounded organic rather than technologic.

Growing up in the melting pot, multicultural sanctuary town of Kotoyeesinay meant hearing just about every human, animal, and magical species vocalization there was, but this was new.

She sat on the road and listened. Singing, maybe? It echoed and resonated like a clarion call.

Throwing off fanciful thoughts, she decided it could be a natural animal. Lots of creatures called to announce territory or when they wanted sex. Hell, even that fool

Fontaine once climbed a tree outside her trailer and made cougar chirps all damn night. Then peed on her porch.

The volume increased. Howling, she decided. It rumbled against her chest, then rose in pitch and made her ears twitch.

It sounded forlorn, like a lost soul. It sounded lonely, like her.

Except she wasn't lonely. She had a loving family and plenty of good friends. Well, none in Florida. And definitely not on Vieques.

Okay, maybe she was a little lonely. She'd always been the odd leopard out. And maybe she'd jumped at the chance to join the exchange program a few years ago because she already knew that no one in her hometown was her mate.

Her tail twitched back and forth, torn as to how to investigate the sound.

Okay, she would compromise. Ordinary human hiker Chantal would walk ten minutes down the road to see what she could see. Then she'd go back to mark the truck location with something visible from the air and head down to the base for reinforcements.

Moments later, she strode briskly eastward. Though she couldn't say why, the need to hurry pressed on her. She topped a rocky rise and stopped in her tracks.

A curved rainbow came from the cloudless sky and plunged into a small lake. Water seemed to slide down the rainbow like a hundred-foot-tall metal wall fountain in a glitzy office building.

At random intervals, water surged and escaped from the rainbow, making loud drips in the pond.

Two sets of wet footprints led away from the pond and over a flat rock, into the scrubby trees on the far side. Human-shaped footprints.

Fairy magic tickled her senses. *Oh, hell.*

Backing away slowly, Chantal spoke quietly. "No intrusion intended. Leaving now." Most fairies, regardless of tribe, were highly territorial and went instantly from zero to lethal if startled. Or insulted. Or interrupted. Or bored.

A faint male voice arrested her. "Help us…" It came from the direction of the footprints.

She couldn't rule out a trap, but she couldn't turn her back on anyone in trouble, either. Besides, all the fairies she'd met would rather die than ask for help.

Calling up her leopard's senses and her best shield spell, she edged warily around the pond that radiated fairy magic.

About thirty steps into the brush, she lost the footprints, but followed a distinct, watery scent.

"Hello?" she called softly. "I'm Deputy… I'm Chantal. How can I help?" She repeated herself in Spanish and French for good measure.

"We're under an acacia tree. Please, my wife needs help." The English was accented, maybe Greek, like Kotoyeesinay's only independent taxi driver.

She could hear and smell them, but even with leopard vision, she couldn't see them. "Sorry, but you'll have to guide me in."

"This way," said a weak, breathy female voice.

Chantal angled north toward the voices and saw a wide, umbrella-like tree with a twisted trunk. The hurricane had done damage, but it still had half its tiny leaves.

She slowed to a halt under the canopy when she heard breathing, and the wet smell intensified. "I have a first-aid kit with me." Taking a chance that they weren't innocent humans who got stuck in a fairy honeypot, she added, "That's a pretty good concealment spell you're using."

"It's wyvern," said the male voice. "We don't know how to remove it."

That explained why it didn't give off a magical signature. Chantal felt forward with one foot, then another, trying to see with her ears and nose. "I have a charm that counters most magic, including wyvern, but it's not gentle." Her toe brushed something unseen and partially vanished. "Is this your spell?"

"Yes, and my foot." said the woman's voice with a touch of asperity.

"Sorry. Want me to try the charm? Or I can radio and have help here in thirty minutes."

The woman's voice started, "I don't–"

"Charm," interrupted the male voice. "The leopard can't help if she can't see. We must run."

"Yes, all right." Exhaustion roughened the woman's tone.

Chantal pulled the flashlight from its holster on her belt. "Cover your eyes. Flash coming in three, two, one…" She focused her intent on the wyvern magic, then pressed and held three innocent-looking buttons on her standard-issue flashlight.

A ghostly net appeared in a sphere shape, then collapsed in a searing flash of light and heat. Two voices cried out in pain.

A naked woman and man appeared, lying on the ground. He cradled her in his arms. Their matted and tangled dark, silver-streaked hair wasn't long enough to hide a multitude of scrapes and cuts that leaked blood. They'd also expelled the unpleasant-smelling contents of their stomachs onto the ground underneath them.

"So bright," said the man, still squinting. His color was looking sallower by the second.

The woman's head shook. "Oh, *Thea*, the smells are even worse!"

Chantal crouched. "I've got a field kit and some healing spells, but–"

An unearthly keening sound interrupted, like the sound of a bomb whistle.

The woman rose to her hands and knees, whimpering, and started to crawl. The man climbed unsteadily to his feet, then bent to help the woman stand. They staggered together east, away from the fairy fountain.

A crashing thump shook the ground hard enough to knock Chantal off balance and send the man to his knees.

The woman pulled the man to his feet. "Get up, Raya. I will not let you be sold!"

Chantal's focus sharpened. Her own mother had been sold as a baby factory to a corrupt pride. The North American shifter community was still untangling the mess left from the destruction of an illegal underground auction operation in California. Chantal had an immediate, visceral dislike for anyone who enslaved and sold shifters like pets.

More thumps, coming closer.

The man and woman pushed into the scraggly bushes.

Chantal pulled a few flashbangs from her belt and stepped out from under the tree.

A huge head rose above the top of a rise to the north, soon joined by more of the creature. It looked like a giant, evil version of a garden gnome. Its head turned a three-quarter rotation, then tilted down to look toward her location. The movement sounded like stones grinding in a rock tumbler. A dust shower of sparkling crystals flew out from the neck.

Another giant figure joined it, this one the nightmare version of a classical satyr, but with a demon's sharp teeth showing through the beard, claws for fingers, and sharp crystal spikes protruding from the goat-half's hooves.

Both appeared to made of cloudy gray quartz, with blocky, rectangular crystals at their joints and around their necks. Uneven blotches of color suggested they'd once been brightly painted. Gusts of powerful fairy magic buffeted her etheric senses.

The quartz satyr squatted, then sprang into the air to land fifty feet down the ridge. The impact shook the ground.

The gnome figure stomped down the hill toward Chantal and the acacia tree. Its booted feet tore and flattened the undergrowth as it stomped toward her.

She sidestepped quickly, away from the tree and into the bushes, exchanging the useless flashbangs for her satellite radio.

"Kitty One to Base. I've got two people hurt. Two twenty-foot animated statues just appeared out of nowhere. I'm about fifteen minutes down the two-wheel track from Road 200. Whole area is thick with fairy magic. I'll try to get the injured to safety and hide. Don't come alone."

No time to wait for the answer. The base receiver would record the message for later playback if Leticia wasn't there.

Reholstering the radio and circling quickly toward where she'd last seen the injured couple, she considered options. The road was too visible. The fairy pool was out of the question.

Best bet would be the mired truck. Metal and modern technology sometimes interfered with fairy magic.

A louder crash shook the ground. The satyr was now only thirty feet from her.

She dove for a bush, twisting at the last second to avoid a cactus. Rolling onto her back, she aimed a magical energy bolt at its neck.

A large, rounded section of hot-pink crystal went flying, bouncing off a tree and landing near her hips. The satyr didn't seem to notice as it stepped closer. The sharp spikes on its hooves had fresh green stains.

The gnome's booted feet stomped forward. The high-pitched keening began again. Communication, maybe?

Her nose detected the watery scent of the couple. She saw the man a moment later, but it was too late.

The gnome scraped away a tree like it was a weed, then reached down with its other clawed hand to scoop him up. A moment later, the satyr did the same to the woman, who screamed in pain when the claws tightened on her ribs.

Chantal froze, not daring to move. The satyr towered over her and her thin cover of shrubbery. One slide of a spiked hoof, and she'd be shifter shish-kabob.

Fairy magic glowed from striations of purple that resembled veins. Visible cracks radiated from all its joints.

She blinked in wonder when she noticed the satyr was anatomically correct with the legendary endowment of that species. Did statues have sex?

Her inner leopard hissed at her to quit thinking stupid human thoughts and pay attention.

Fairy magic flared, followed by the unmistakable blossoming of demesne magic.

"Leopard!" shouted the man. "Tell the Cypriot capricorns that Rayapkhal and Yipkash are not dead! Look for buyers who–"

The rest of his words were swallowed by the deafening wind of a fairy portal opening. Twenty feet from Chantal's hiding place, the air shimmered, then stabilized. The morning sun over Vieques cast a wide spotlight onto a dark world of thick trees, lit dimly by small floating globes.

The portal stretched taller and wider, creeping to within a body's length from her.

The garden gnome thunder-stomped through the opening. The round, pink crystal at its neck flared bright with raw fairy magic.

Right above her, the satyr's head rotated three hundred

and sixty degrees. A shower of tiny crystals coated her as it turned.

The satyr stepped one hoof through the opening, then paused. More fairy magic bathed it up and down. The woman cried out in pain.

Intuition and impulse hit Chantal at the same time. She grabbed the round pink crystal that had almost hit her, then tucked and rolled with it through the portal, under the satyr's hoof spikes.

Fairy magic scoured every inch of her. The pink crystal rapidly became too hot to handle and seared her hands and upper chest. She hung on to it with grim determination.

Gritting her teeth, she raised her magic shield. The portal defense magic—that's what it had to be—stopped needling her nerves. Ahead of her, human screams shifted into bleating goat sounds. She scrambled to her feet and ran for the thick forest.

This was either the luckiest or stupidest thing she'd ever done. But how could she live with herself if it was another auction?

The pink crystal continued to glow, but cooled off enough for her to stuff it down her shirt, resting on the camisole. She welcomed the noticeably cooler air of the demesne. The portal shut with another pop of rushing air.

As she moved as quickly and quietly as possible into the shadows of larger trees, the profound lack of scents disturbed her. Faint whiffs of what could be pine, but that was it. Not even her own sweat. Maybe the portal defense magic evaporated it.

The etheric vibration of the portal subsided. Stomps and clomp sounds headed away from her to the left, so she turned that direction.

A strong temptation to shift to full leopard form pushed her, but she doubted she could magically shift the pink crystal with her clothes, and it was too big to carry in her leopard's mouth. She'd be a fool to lose the crystal, and her parents didn't raise fools.

But they were going to be mad. She'd promised them that just this once, she'd try to stay out of trouble instead of jumping into it.

She vowed to make it up to them. If she survived.

5

Dauro sprawled on the cool floor of the castle's great hall, forelimbs outstretched. He should be outside, finding out what happened when two of the castle's statues opened a portal to chase the escaped capricorns. Instead, he was stuck inside, commanded to appear before the new owners.

He'd expected punishment for making all that noise, but they hadn't said a thing. Instead, they were conducting more magical experiments.

The two fairies stood behind a long, narrow table with random stones, charms, and magical instruments scattered across it. They'd also bedecked themselves with chains and rings of gold. Dauro recognized some of them from Nessireth's various collections.

The display cases in the hall now gaped open, some with broken doors. Nessireth used to bring him into the castle every year for a checkup and to brag about new acquisitions. Toward the end of her life, the inspections had come more frequently and she'd grown more garrulous, as if she'd wanted someone to talk to.

Or maybe she'd forgotten he had a brain under all his fur.

"Okay," said Trixis. "Let's try the change wand."

The taller fairy named Omorachi picked up a slender length of carved crystal and pointed it at him. He didn't recognize it. Trixis read a passage from the book they'd been carrying the day before.

Their previous experiments had fizzled or failed, but this time, Trixis's last syllable set Dauro free.

Mind-ripping pain coursed through him. Magic tore him apart, limb by limb, then remade him. Feet, knees, hands, stomach, lungs, head. His roar of agony became a human shout. Long ago, his shifts had taken less than a dozen heartbeats. This one felt like it took hours.

He sagged on his hands and knees in a chilly puddle. The water from his fur must have drained off during the shift. The face reflecting back up at him was that of an unkempt stranger. He'd always looked different, with a short beard that native males didn't have, but had his hair always been that thick and full of dark and silver coils?

Omorachi wrinkled her nose and fanned the air in front of her face. "Ugh! Humans bloody well stink! No wonder Nessie kept 'em as animals."

"That," declared Trixis, "was the most disgusting thing I've ever seen in my life." She pointed at something to his right. "Cover your lumpy brown flesh before I throw up."

Dauro peered blearily up at them. He wasn't used to looking up at anything, or seeing in full color. Every muscle and bone in his body hurt like hot knives.

Trixis made a retching sound and pointed again.

He turned to look. A faded red blanket draped over a threadbare padded green chair that was twenty feet away. Instead of trusting his uncertain balance, he awkwardly crawled to the chair. The rough-surfaced, milky-white quartz floor sliced into the tender skin on his hands and knees, leaving a trail of water and blood in his wake.

Omorachi made a scoffing noise. "I saw a python eat a goblin once. Snake died of poison. Goblin ate its way out. That's way worse."

"Hmph." Trixis examined the wand in her hand, then put it back on the table. "At least this one works like it's supposed to. It'll bring a good price."

"So, foul-smelling creature," said Omorachi loudly, "what's your name?"

Dauro wasn't born on the vegetable truck yesterday. Names had power. He gave them his war leader title instead. "Sinchi."

Embarrassingly, his voice was rusty, and he drooled as he spoke the unfamiliar sounds of English. His tongue felt short and entirely the wrong shape. His numb lips didn't help. Congestion clogged his nose and ears. The hall seemed darker than he remembered, and drafty.

He rolled to sit on the floor, leaning against the chair, and pulled the thin blanket around his shoulders. It was a poor replacement for thick fur.

Omorachi thumped the table in annoyance. "If Nessie was here, I'd slap her. Her precious 'Book of Books' is full of shite." She waved toward the table. "Or more to the point, *not* full of it. Half this isn't even listed, or if it is, it's a lie."

Trixis took a sip of blue liquid from a clear crystal goblet. "Untrusting rubble, she was." She held up the glass. "Look how long it took us to break into the fairy dew cellar, and we're her flesh and stone."

"Stop drinking so much." Omorachi's expression turned sour. "Half of that is mine."

Trixis rolled her shoulders back. "I deserve more. I'm still growing."

"Lick hot lava," Omorachi snarled. "I'm the one who figured out where Nessie hid the demesne and got us in."

Trixis defiantly drained the goblet, then slammed it to the table. "Yeah, well, I'm the one who found the sales broker for the collection."

"On the *human* internet," Omorachi sneered. "You haven't even met her. She could be a scammer."

"I talked to her. That's enough. Our project isn't going anywhere without money."

"*Our* project?" Omorachi screeched in outrage. "You'd still be pounding granite in your mother's quarry if it weren't for me." Omorachi punched Trixis on the arm.

Trixis punched back, but missed Omorachi's arm and grazed her jaw.

The next instant, they were punching, biting, and scratching each other.

When their scuffle bumped the table, the contents flew off and landed on the floor. Several pieces rolled toward him.

He'd forgotten how much more sensitive to magic he was in his human form. The box with dull pebbles glued to it had a tiny glamor to make them look like precious gems. The oversized iron key had no magic. On the other hand, the slender knife with the dragon-scale hilt was bespelled Alfar metal designed to cut through anything. In his time, only leaders of big clans could afford such a deadly weapon.

Quickly, before the fairies ended their scuffle, he wrapped his hand in the blanket and pushed the knife behind him under the chair. With luck, the fairies wouldn't find it for a while.

Magic thrummed through the floor. His human physical senses were even worse than he'd remembered, but four hundred years of living in fairy magic had honed his magical senses sharp.

The castle's unique magic was strong and complex. Nessireth often boasted she alone had figured out how to fuse fairy magic to living rock to give the castle autonomy to protect her and her collections. Now that he was sitting —huddling, to be honest—inside, he believed it. The castle's power vibrated his bones.

Demesne magic floated everywhere. It felt as torn and threadbare as the blanket around his shoulders. Whatever plan the squabbling fairies had for their inheritance, they'd best repair the demesne soon or lose it altogether.

He wished Sunscar would let him know what was happening outside. Or maybe ignorance was better, so he couldn't give it away if the fairies found Nessireth's favorite truth-geas ring.

Stretching out his legs, he wiggled his toes and flexed his feet. How odd to have so many short toes.

He dimly remembered his first shift to his sloth, centuries ago, and how nothing felt right. Of course, part of that was because he'd expected to be an elephant seal like his parents, not a huge, furry, long-snouted, four-legged vegetarian with claws for digging up underwater plants. He hadn't known what to call himself until Nessireth had bragged to a visitor that he was a unique and valuable Ice Age aquatic sloth. Megafauna, she'd called him.

Valuable to collectors, maybe, but shifter clans hadn't known what to do with him any more than his parents had. Becoming good at war made him useful but not loved, except by the other warriors.

The fairies' fight ended as abruptly as it started. They picked themselves up off the floor and straightened their torn clothing as if nothing happened. Thanks to Kelvin's borrowed memories, he now knew the shorter Trixis wore skinny jeans and a T-shirt, and taller Omorachi wore leggings under a short skirt and chain-covered vest.

They righted the table, then picked up the book and the empty goblet.

"Sinchi!" said Trixis, her nose in the air. "Pick up this mess you made." She pointed toward the scattered items on the floor. Omorachi snickered and crossed her arms expectantly.

Ordinarily, he'd have told them to eat death leaves, but not this time. He needed information more than he needed his dignity. Letting the blanket drop, he used the chair for support as he rose unsteadily to his feet.

After two cautious steps, he decided that thinking about walking on two legs only made it worse, so he concentrated on wanting to touch the charms and find out what they did. Keeping his movements sloth-slow helped him master bending and straightening, but his limbs were barely speaking to each other. And to think he'd regularly outraced the fastest runners of his long-ago clan.

Trixis and Omorachi hooted and hissed laughter every time he stumbled. Their inattentiveness helped him conceal a small, powerful pearl in his mouth. Now he just had to remember not to forget and reflexively swallow it.

By the time he'd made a dozen trips to the table, he almost felt like his body was his own again, even if everything still ached.

"Let's take pictures of him now," demanded Trixis. "I don't want to have to smell him any longer than I have to."

"Fine." Omorachi heaved an aggrieved sigh. "I'll get my phone. Ask him about the others." She spun and walked toward an arched doorway, her clawed toenails clicking on the stone.

Trixis put her hands on her hips. "Where is the *Draco aqua?*"

"The what?" His voice sounded smoother, but the words sounded weird. Maybe it was the English language Sunscar had given him, not at all like Spanish. Come to think of it, old Nessireth had boasted to everyone that the demesne acted as a universal translator. Which explained why he'd understood the fairies from the beginning. Very confusing, nonetheless.

Trixis opened the book and flipped pages, then turned it to show him. "This." The sketches showed Rosinette, the sea wyvern, with the chained rods that pierced her wings.

He squinted at the page, wishing Sunscar's magic had included teaching him to read fairy script. "In her habitat?"

Trixis stomped her foot. "No, she's not. We tried both the pool and the tree grove. Where else?"

He blinked sloth-slow and made a show of puzzlement. "I only know the river." The pearl under his tongue nearly made him drool again.

Trixis made a crunching sound with her teeth. "Is she *in* the river?" Her tone was that of an impatient adult to an inattentive toddler.

"I don't know. I'm not in the river now." Risky to play that stupid, but he was counting on Nessireth's book to not have mentioned that any of her collection had brains. Forcing them to keep their non-talking animal forms meant she didn't have to feel guilty about it.

"Okay, how about the eel? Or the swimming cat?" She flipped a page and pointed to illustrations of the capricorns. "Or whatever these animals are. None of them are where she marked them on the map."

He shook his head. "I'm not allowed to–"

The castle shuddered under his feet. Demesne magic burned like wind-blown embers on his tender human skin. The goblet on the table tipped over.

"Castle, what are you doing?" Trixis yelled angrily.

The castle's voice, seeming to come from nowhere and

everywhere, sounded irritated. "The demesne refuses entry to a retriever."

Omorachi arrived, carrying her phone. "Why does a dog want into the demesne?"

"The retriever is mine," the castle declared.

"Oh, great. The castle has a pet." Trixis wrinkled her nose. "Something else to stink up the place."

The shaking intensified. The charms on the table danced with the vibration.

Omorachi spread her arms wide and shouted. "Demesne, I order you–"

The shaking stopped.

Omorachi smiled triumphantly and dropped her arms. "I'm brilliant."

Trixis rolled her eyes. "Take the photos. Nessie's book has all kinds of warnings about keeping the collection apart, but if they're all as witless as this one, we won't have to bother." She frowned. "We'll have to finesse that in the sales copy or their defects will depress the price."

"After we get the pics, let's go ahead and put the collection all in one place. The hell with Nessie's warning. Maybe we'll get a discount when the shifter wranglers get here. Which reminds me." She held out her arms again. "I, Omorachi, rightful heir to this demesne and castle, hereby order you to let the wranglers in without any faffing about."

"Hey! I'm an heir, too!" said Trixis. She raised her arms to match Omorachi's pose. "I order you to let them in and be nice to them, too."

Omorachi glared at Trixis, then turned her attention to her phone. Circling Dauro, she took quite a few flash pictures. "Maybe we should put him in some human clothes so he looks normal."

Trixis made a rude noise. "Clothes can't fix ugly. Nothing would fit over those overgrown shoulders and thighs. Anyway, shifters go naked all the time. Like old Nessie did."

Omorachi grinned evilly. "Maybe all her extra magic was because she was a secret shifter."

"Ewww—gross!" shrieked Trixis. "No wonder some tribes still kill half-breeds."

"Bloody well right." Omorachi picked up the slender change wand. "If we're done with him, let's turn him back for now. Humans are rank." Her lips and nose wrinkled in disgust. "Besides, the water cat can't have gone far with that chain."

Trixis flipped pages in the book. "Okay, but let's make the castle statues carry her. Water makes my hair stick out." Pointing the wand and reading from the book, she rattled off the spell.

Pain hit hard as the shift magic took hold and remade him again. He barely remembered not to bite down on the pearl in his mouth as his jawbone grew, along with the rest of him.

After a long minute, he lay on the floor, exhausted and hurting. Silver threads of shifter magic danced in his peripheral vision. Hunger gnawed at his suddenly hollow stomach.

"Out!" Omorachi waved her hands toward the door. "Don't make me push your fat arse!"

He lurched up on four familiar paws and padded clumsily out the huge castle entryway, past the gravel and onto the lawn.

It was coming up on false dawn. Ordinarily, he didn't need the demesne's floating lights to see by, but right now, he'd take all the help he could get. Even his eyelids hurt.

He plodded toward the river, head drooping, claws dragging in the grass.

Finally, the willing water embraced him, soothing his aches as it carried him to his riverine den.

He stashed his new treasure, longing for the dexterity of his human self. They'd need Sunscar in his wraith form to use it, but the pearl was their best chance of getting free. Hopefully, the fairies wouldn't miss it anytime soon.

He needed to eat before he passed out.

Find Sunscar.

Free the others.

Escape.

Oblivion took him instead.

6

Chantal's experience with the fairy demesnes anchored around Kotoyeesinay gave her an idea of what to expect. But she'd never been in an empty one before.

Okay, not empty, because she was following animated statues that carried piteously bleating capricorns in vice-like grips. And at the edge of the forest, she'd seen a pygmy hippopotamus try to trip the gnome statue and get cruelly kicked for its trouble.

It was more like the demesne was unclaimed, which she hadn't thought possible. Demesnes were fantasy lands that sprung from the will and magical strength of the fairy who created them.

Dawn suddenly lit the landscape like a grow-lamp on a timer. The independent mage lights that floated everywhere dimmed.

But no time to think about that now, because the hippo was hurting and the statues were marching away fast.

The demesne energized her magical senses, so she knew the hippo was a male shifter. She didn't think he was bleeding, but she couldn't be sure. Her sense of smell had become suddenly unreliable, like she'd been sneezing from a snoot-full of pollen. The moment she'd crossed through the portal, her nose shut down.

Edging out from behind a tree near where the hippo lay panting, she spoke softly. "Hi, there."

Her attempt at not scaring him failed miserably. Scrambling to his feet, he squeaked in fear and threat, backing away from her.

She stepped farther away from the tree, holding up her hands so he could see she had no weapons. "I'm Chantal, leopard shifter. I know a healing spell or two that can make you feel better."

The hippo's warning huff and show of teeth froze her in place. He could mow her down before she had a chance to shift.

She sighed. "I hope you understand English or Spanish, or we're going to be here a while."

He nodded slowly, which encouraged her.

"I'm not here to hurt anyone. I just want to find out what happened to the capricorns, Yipkash and Rayapkhal. I found them outside, injured. When the statues opened a portal and took them inside the demesne, I followed." She gave him a self-deprecating smile. "Probably not the smartest thing I've ever done, but here I am."

The hippo grunted and sat on his haunches.

She dropped her hands slowly. "If you don't trust me to heal you, maybe you can shift–"

The hippo's head shook vigorously from side to side.

"Okay then. Can you at least point me in the right direction to find the capricorns? I promised I'd help them."

The hippo crouched and whined.

Like their natural counterparts, shifted animals didn't

have words or facial expressions, but she followed her hunch. "You want me to heal you?"

At the hippo's nod, she moved slowly toward him. "I'll bet both your sides hurt."

Once she got close enough to kneel next to his shoulders, she decided he was probably a juvenile rather than full grown. She'd seen natural pygmy hippos in online videos, and the adults looked fatter and darker. "Is it all right if I touch you?"

He answered by rolling into her outstretched hand. The contact instantly told her his wet, greenish-black skin hid the big bruise she could feel with her energized magical senses. The bruise on his other side was worse, where the gnome statue's boot had sent him flying. Young shifters with inexperienced magical immune systems took longer to heal.

"I'm going to use a stronger spell. It'll feel like your skin is on fire for about ten seconds, and then like you're in an ice bath. After that, you'll want to eat everything in sight." She patted his shoulder. "Preferably not me."

Narrowing her focus to her intent, she spoke the cantrip in her mind. Demesne magic tried to embellish her shifter magic spell, but she gently nudged it aside. The young hippo didn't need a layer of diamond armor added to his flanks.

Keeping her hand on him, she made soothing noises as the spell's hot and cold phases took their course. The bruises cleared up and the cracked rib remade itself, as if he'd shifted. He'd still be sore for a few hours, but at least it wouldn't be days.

"Okay, kid, you can get up now. Moving will help you get warm. At least I hope you're a kid, or I owe you an apology." Shifter magic threads danced in the air at the edge of her peripheral vision. The demesne's magic provided more threads to complement the movements. Whoever created the demesne deserved respect for how much free potential it had.

Rising to her feet carefully, because that spell always made her lightheaded, she wiped her damp hand on her khaki pants, leaving a pinkish smear. At least they were still pants. Some demesnes magically enforced a dress code in keeping with the owner's preference. Fluttery dresses made of flower petals never had pockets.

The hippo pushed to his feet and took a couple of bouncing steps that shook his rounded torso.

The edge of a pink-tinged arc appeared on the horizon to her right. All the mage lights extinguished. The simulated sunrise was better than some she'd seen, but lacked the subtle color variations and clouds of the real world.

Water sounds caught her attention. At least whatever was wrong with her sense of smell wasn't affecting her ears. "Am I hearing a river?"

The hippo nodded. He took a few steps toward it, then turned and tilted his head.

"Sorry, but I can't go play with you right now. I need to find the capricorns."

The hippo grunted and nodded, then tilted his head again.

"Oh, you're taking me to them?" She frowned, looking across the landscape in the direction she'd last seen the statues. She'd been lucky so far. Better to go with the hippo she knew than the demesne she didn't.

She had to admit that for once, she was lost. The only thing she knew to do was create a map in her head as she followed the little hippo over the uneven ground. She assigned the direction of the artificial sunrise as east. That put the forest behind her to the north, the river south, and the wide expanse of rock-strewn flat land to the west.

Eastward, the flatland rose to rolling green hills with more rocks and a few flowers. Hard to tell how far it went. Demesnes could only simulate the physics of the real world, and most fairies didn't bother.

An abrupt downward slope gave her a view of the bluest river she'd ever seen. Easily half a mile wide and flowing westward. Waves and ripples dominated the center. At the shore, the water lapped on sand and rocks. About a hundred yards to her right, a diverted section of the river formed a turquoise lake area around a small island populated with trees. Above the far shore rose an eroded, chalky-white cliff that plunged into green water.

The hippo took several steps into the shallows. A moment later, he squealed and lunged back on the bank, scrambling toward her.

From out of the river rose the figure of a naked, tattooed black man, as if formed by the water itself. Sinuously handsome, with strong features, and long, silver dreadlocks flowing down his back like twisting snakes. His glowing red eyes drilled into hers.

"Who are you?" His deep, rumbling bass vibrated her chest. He radiated fury and vengeance.

The hippo put himself in front of her, with his butt touching her thigh. He trembled, but stood his ground.

She narrowed her eyes at the wraith in disapproval. "You're scaring my friend."

Silver eyebrows rose above red eyes. "Young Kelvin is susceptible. But not you?"

"Nope. One of my mother's clients is a corporeal wraith like you." She shrugged. "Runs a diner. I bussed tables during the summer tourist seasons."

He blinked several times, looking stunned. Finally, he crossed his arms. "Why are you here?" His English was accented, but she couldn't place it.

"Looking for new friends." She jutted her chin in subtle challenge. "You?"

His head nodded toward Kelvin. "Looking out for old ones." After a long moment, his arms dropped and his expression softened. "He tells me you healed him. I am Sunscar. The demesne belongs to… used to belong to a rock fairy named Nessireth. She died two months ago. Her kin arrived two days ago and mean to sell us all for money."

It was her turn to blink. "Who is us?"

"Her collection of exotic aquatic shifters." Magic pulsed as tattoos on his chest lit up for a moment.

She raised an eyebrow. "You're a shifter?"

Kelvin fairly glowed with shifter magic, but none came from Sunscar.

"I am an abomination created by a monster who sold me to Nessireth as a novelty. My animal form is a giant eel." His bleak tone was at odds with the challenging jut of his chin.

"Created? By the infamous dark elf known as Surasa, by chance?" She shook her head. "Never mind, none of my business and way above my pay grade." She pointed toward the island and cliffs. "Kelvin is taking me to the capricorns. I promised to help them."

Sunscar's expression softened. "Did they get out to the real world?"

"Yes, but not for long. I think the statues fetched them back. I slipped in when they opened the portal." She opened her shirt to show him the top part of the pink crystal. "They dropped this."

He glanced, then stared, eyes wide. "You need to talk to everyone." He pointed westward as he began to sink into the water. "Kelvin, take her to the bridge immediately. I will awaken Dauro and summon all the others." Just before his head disappeared, he drilled her with a stern look. "Do not shift."

After a few seconds of splashy churning, she got a glimpse of a huge, pale eel with a rounded mouth full of teeth and the same wraith-red eyes. He disappeared into the river.

She stepped around the hippo to look at his face. "Can we trust him?"

Kelvin hesitated a long moment, then nodded his head slowly, with apparent reluctance.

"Okay, then." She frowned. "He's free with the orders, though. You don't have to go if you don't want to."

Snorting, Kelvin headed westward, along the transition strip between the orderly sparse grasses and the equally orderly river bank.

Turning, she walked briskly behind the hippo. She would comply with the "don't shift" order for the time being. Demesnes often had whimsical rules that went beyond dress codes. She didn't fancy being turned into a miniature stegosaurus or something.

Kelvin kept turning his head toward her, as if anxious.

"We can go faster, if you want. But you need to eat soon. That spell ate up your reserves." Not to mention some of her own. Bad luck that she'd skipped breakfast to hike up the island road.

He nodded and picked up the pace. She sped up to a slow jog.

The river was more like a giant, landscaped water feature than a natural occurrence, which made for easy traveling beside its channelized banks. The demesne magic that controlled the water and made it flow pushed against her senses, sparking her creativity, teasing her to play.

Pay attention, she told herself. *Make magic arts-and-crafts projects later.*

It took forty minutes by her reckoning to come within

sight of their destination. Assuming time worked like it did in the real world, which wasn't always a given.

Her inner leopard was getting grumpy. Cats preferred to leave long-distance running to wolves. She took a long drink from her charmed canteen, which would replenish itself after a few minutes.

The river narrowed considerably and became deeper blue in this part, likely due to an increase in depth. A bridge with elaborate decorative carvings spanned this section and looked solid enough to handle elephants.

The castle beyond had a hodge-podge of architectural elements, from crenelated turrets to many tiny conical roofs. At least a dozen giant-sized statues decorated the front lawn, no two alike. She had to assume the huge evil garden gnome was the same one that had captured the capricorns. Even though Kelvin ignored them, she kept a watchful eye on the statues.

Moving closer to the bridge felt like approaching a bonfire. The bridge radiated various flavors of layered magic, only about half of which she recognized. Shifter magic intensified, too, telling her other shifters were nearby.

When Kelvin plunged into the water, she stayed on the sandy bank. She drew the line at swimming fully clothed in water that felt as alive with magic as the bridge.

Almost immediately, Sunscar rose from the water in the shadow of the bridge.

"Can you speak mind to mind?" His deep bass voice echoed off the stone.

"I'm still learning." Which was to say, she avoided it. Telepathy hadn't come nearly as easily to her as using her free magic, and she liked her privacy.

"I can help, if you give me permission." He shrugged one shoulder. "It is my gift."

The thought made her uneasy, but she didn't see another choice. "Okay, but no snooping in the lingerie drawers."

Pressure expanded in her head, then released like an air-pressure change. She swallowed hard.

Welcome to our party. Sunscar sent her names and three-dimensional images of his friends underwater. Kelvin, floating near the surface. Yipkash and Rayapkhal, the two capricorns, tails intertwined. Nibi, a feline covered with copper-colored fish scales, chained to an underwater pillar. Rosinette, a sea wyvern leaking blood from pierced and hobbled wings.

And Dauro, an Ice Age aquatic sloth the size of an elephant, with a long, wide snout, beaver-brown shaggy fur that fluttered in the current, and huge claws dug into the bank as anchors.

Thank you for trying to help us. That was the female capricorn named Yipkash. *You've put yourself in terrible danger.*

Chantal opened her mouth to reply, then had to remind herself to use her thoughts instead. *It's in the job description. Are you hurt? I have healing spells.*

She healed me after the gnome kicked me, said Kelvin. *It didn't hurt much.*

We were healed by the forced shift, said Rayapkhal, the other capricorn. He wasn't good at hiding his stress.

No offense intended, said Nibi, *but you have to be more than a leopard shifter. Otherwise, the pink quartz crystal you carry would burn you as fast as the Alfar chains would burn me if I shifted to human.*

Chantal sent the group a thread of amusement. *No offense taken. I'm a melting pot. On my mother's side, I'm human from a long line of witches, plus fairy, elf, and kitsune. As to my sperm donor's side... They tout their pure leopard heritage, but* they probably invented the phrase "catting around." *A lot of outcrosses like me aren't on the official family tree.*

Can you feel the demesne magic? Dauro's question held a note of hope. *Maybe a better question is, can you use it?*

Of course she can, said Rosinette, *or she'd never have made it past the portal.* Even in mind speech, Chantal could hear the unique wyvern accent, which had an undercurrent of music.

I can feel it, Chantal admitted, *but I mostly get by on instinct. Fairies aren't patient teachers, and I'm a youngling by their standards. I know it energizes some kinds of other magic, like shifter or wraith. To be honest, I don't know why your demesne didn't collapse when its creator died.*

Nessireth was millennia old, said Dauro. *Her tribe rejected her because she liked to show off her prodigious magic. She poured all her power into building the demesne to protect herself, then to flaunt her skill. The collections came later. She craved being envied.*

Telepathically, Dauro had one of those voices she could listen to all day. If he'd been her instructor instead of an irascible vampire, she might have enjoyed the lessons.

I'm flattered, Dauro replied with good-natured humor, *but as a sloth, I'm limited.*

Sorry, she sent, along with embarrassment. *I'll try not to overshare.*

A wave of amusement came from Nibi. *We've all done it. We're beginners compared to Sunscar.*

They teach classes in magic and telepathy in the world these days? asked Sunscar.

Sanctuary towns and hidden institutes do, Chantal replied. *Not in the rest of the world. Humans only believe in science.*

Yipkash spoke up. *We brought our treasure.* She sent an image of a bracelet and a heavy charm. *They have magic, but we don't know what. Nessireth cursed when she threw them in the river, so they may not be useful.*

I don't have anything. Kelvin's small voice sounded dejected.

Chantal focused a soothing thought toward him, but couldn't tell if it worked. If she survived this adventure, she planned to find a better telepathy teacher. One with a soothing mental voice.

My treasure isn't a thing, it's knowledge, said Rosinette. *I memorized every spell she ever used within my hearing. The suppressor magic in the wing hobble means I can't speak them, but I can teach others.*

Excellent, said Dauro. *You are very clever.*

I do what I can. Rosinette's modest words belied the pleasure she took in Dauro's praise.

Mine is knowledge, too. Nibi's words held satisfaction. *Nessireth pretended the castle is the demesne's heart, but it's not. It's this bridge. I nearly escaped four times. It's the only thing strong enough to hold me captive. We have an understanding of sorts.*

Very interesting, thought Sunscar, with sincerity. *My contribution is also...*

Chantal's inner leopard twitched and demanded she look toward the castle.

Hell. One of the statues was stepping down off its pedestal. A smaller one was already moving toward the river. And there she stood, gawking like a summer tourist.

Striding hurriedly toward the bridge, hoping to find someplace under it to hide, she sent the others a mental snapshot of what she'd seen.

You won't make it in time. Step in the water and stay still, said Rosinette. *I will hide you.*

Chantal threw aside her misgivings about the magic-charged river and waded in. It was colder than she liked, but not unbearable. Unpleasant tendrils of wetness infiltrated her boots via her socks.

A flare of wyvern magic settled on her, like the net that had been around the human-shifted capricorns. She was grateful to be hidden, but she felt completely exposed, standing there. A close observer would notice where her legs disrupted the water flow, but hunkering down would only make it worse.

Remorse came from Dauro. *I think Omorachi and Trixis want Nibi. I meant to warn you, but I fell asleep.*

I can't hide you all, said Rosinette. *We'll have to separate.*

They won't bother the rest of you if I'm on the usual ledge in plain sight, said Nibi. *Why do they want me?*

Pictures, replied Dauro. *Questions. Maybe to try magic objects. They used a new force-shifter on me twice.* He sent an image of a crystal wand. *They're reading from the book Nessireth kept, but they don't know what they're doing.*

About a hundred feet from Chantal, under the bridge, a copper-scaled cougar climbed onto a thick ledge that circled one of the bridge's sturdy piers. Nibi walked toward the outer side of the bridge until the chain pulled taut, then crouched on all fours. The Alfar metal chain glowed even in the shadows. A heavy lock rested across her shoulders, keeping the Alfar harness tight. Even from that distance, Chantal felt its lethal magic. No wonder Nibi was afraid of it.

I hate that book, said Nibi. *She used her truth-geas ring to make me tell her my name and history so she could write it down. Gloated the whole time like she was counting diamonds.*

You aren't the only one she did that to. The information in that book could kill us all. Sunscar's bleak declaration silenced them for a long moment.

The taller statue, a malformed, hunchback version of a forest giant—humans insultingly called them Bigfoot—

stepped onto the bridge. The shorter statue of a malevolent fanged and clawed cherub followed.

They opened their mouths in unison. A booming female voice emanated from both at once, like stereo speakers.

"Swimming cat shifter. Come with the statues to the castle."

She can't! thought Kelvin. *The chains!*

Those clusterfucking fairies will kill her. Cold anger iced Sunscar's words.

"Oh, bloody hell," a higher-pitched voice with a British accent emanated from the open-mouthed statues, "the book says she's *under* the bridge and we need a key for the harness. Nessie added a walkway to go visit her."

"I'll get the box," came a lower voice.

Nibi, what does the key look like? asked Dauro.

Big gray crystal top, Alfar metal shaft and bit, maybe ten inches long. Nessireth wore it on a heavy necklace whenever I saw it. Her tail switched in agitation.

Nothing like that was on the table. Dauro shared an image of a long, thin table with magical artifacts haphazardly scattered across it. *About a third of them felt magical. I was only able to hide the Alfar knife and steal Nessireth's portal pearl before they changed me back.*

What!? demanded Sunscar angrily. *Why didn't you tell us?*

He just did, pointed out Chantal, irritated by Sunscar's lack of empathy. *Maybe you're immune, but even for Ice Age shifters, being unnaturally force-shifted just once is like being run over by a tank. I'm impressed he's even coherent.*

Don't mind Sunscar, said Dauro. *He thinks he can't leave when the rest of us escape. It makes him depressed.*

A flurry of mixed emotions came from Sunscar, too fast for Chantal to follow.

"Found it!" The British-accented voice exclaimed from the open-mouthed statues. "Here. Go unlock it."

"No, you go," said the lower-pitched voice. "I'm tired of doing all the work around here while you drink all the dew."

"Fine. We'll go together." The British voice sounded testy. "That way you won't nick more things while I'm gone."

"Fine!" boomed the lower-pitched voice. "But I haven't stolen anything. You probably lost it."

"Shut up."

"No, you shut up!"

The mouths snapped closed and the statues went inert. If Chantal hadn't seen the statues in action before, she might have mistaken them for just weirdly-placed yard art.

Rosinette, asked Chantal, *am I invisible to rock fairies?*

The wyvern's long hesitation didn't inspire confidence. *You should be, as long as you're in the water.*

I'll conceal her, said Dauro. *We need her demesne magic.*

Seconds later, a long, brown snout appeared above the surface of the water. *You should back up. I'm big.*

Chantal backpedaled onto the bank, keeping half of one water-logged boot in the water.

The size and heft of his sloth amazed her. She'd seen smaller dragons. His wavy, beaver-like fur quickly shed water as he lumbered up the bank. The triple claws on his front and rear paws were easily three feet long. No ears, but whiskers on his muzzle and huge, mesmerizing blue-green eyes, the color of a tropical island sea.

He moved closer. *If it's all right with you, I'll wrap around you and pretend to be napping.*

Yes. Will you be okay? She appreciated his protection, but she'd seen what the statues could do.

Yes. He sent an image of a tiny, frustrated fairy struggling to push his wide hindquarters.

After a bit of grunting effort, he settled his elephant-sized bulk half in and half out of the water, with his belly facing away from the water.

Keeping a watchful eye toward the statues, she stepped carefully into the middle of him. He curled his limbs slowly toward her.

Movement near the castle galvanized her into ducking and half lying on one of his muscular limbs, and rolling into his broad, damp chest.

The physical contact immediately amplified their telepathic connection. Shifter magic threads lit up. *I'm not hurting you?*

No. You're like holding a kitten. Humor colored his thoughts.

She smothered a chuckle. *I promise not to bite.* Relaxing into his wet warmth was easier than she'd imagined. *Which reminds me, why did Sunscar tell me not to shift?*

The demesne keeps us permanently as animals so we can't speak or work magic. He was probably worried you wouldn't be able to shift back to human.

Wow. She couldn't even guess what it must be like never to shift. *Nessireth must have been going for induction into the Ancient Asshole Hall of Fame.*

A distressingly high number of Kotoyeesinay residents had horrific experiences with collectors and the hunters who supplied them. The whole heinous industry royally pissed her off.

With her nose practically buried in his fur, she could finally smell something. He had an unexpectedly mossy, peppery, almost mineral scent. Her inner leopard wanted to roll all over him.

Sternly warning her leopard that giant sloths were not catnip toys to drool on, she cast about for something else to think about. *If you don't mind my asking, how long have you been here?*

Four hundred years, more or less. Nessireth said the demesne keeps real time. The last I saw of the real world, the Spanish invaders were decimating the human tribes and empires of South America. Their sorcerers destroyed the last mixed shifter clan and sold most of the defeated warriors into slavery. Me, they sold to Nessireth. He blew out a long breath. With her head against his wide chest, it sounded like a wind tunnel. *Sunscar is very talented in the mental arts. He taught me English and gave most of us context memories from young Kelvin so our ignorance wouldn't kill us if we ever get out of here. But there is so much I still don't understand.*

A near-overwhelming impulse to comfort him warred with a fiery desire to resurrect Nessireth and haul her and her demesne to Kotoyeesinay for exacting judgment. *I came here to help the capricorns, but I'm expanding my mission to include you all.*

Thank you. Relief threaded through his thoughts and through the haze of shifter magic that surrounded him. *I am doing all I can to free them. None of them deserve this.*

The depth of love in his words moved her. *You don't, either.* Unexpected tears filled her eyes. Luckily, no one was there to see. *Everyone should have an ally like you.*

Whatever he might have said was interrupted by the arrival of the fairies.

"Oy! Swimming cat!" came the high-pitched British accent Chantal recognized from the statues . "Where are you?"

Nibi, crouched on her ledge, yowled. Anyone who spoke feline would recognize the irritation in her tone.

"This river bank smells like ass," came the other now-familiar voice.

Chantal asked Dauro what the fairies looked like. In the image he shared, they were barefoot, claw-toed teens dressed like they were going through a Goth phase.

However, based on their independence, they had to be several centuries old. Fairies were odd.

"Look," shouted the lower-pitched voice with alarm. "It's the fat sloth. Is he dead?"

That one's name is Trixis, explained Dauro. In Chantal's mind, Dauro pictured the shorter fairy.

"No," said the British-accented voice, "his ribs are moving. Where are the stairs for the walkway?"

That's Omorachi, said Dauro. *She takes pictures with her cell phone.*

"Over here, by the column. Why couldn't Nessireth collect something smaller and easier to sell, like soul stars or phoenix ash?"

"A sharp stone in the ass, she was," agreed Omorachi.

Chantal's sensitive hearing picked out the sounds of scraping. She imagined fairy claws on stone.

After long minutes of scraping, Omorachi squealed. "There she is! At least she's pretty."

"Yeah, but she stinks worse than the sloth," said Trixis. "Let's make the statues walk her in."

Chantal nudged Dauro. *Don't listen to them. I think you smell great.*

Thank you, Dauro replied, amused. *So do you.*

"Fine." Omorachi sounded long suffering. "The book says she's an escape artist, so I won't unlock her until they get here."

Moments later, the unmistakable sound of statue-stomping drowned out the continued conversation.

I should have faced the water, said Dauro, *so we could see what they're doing.*

I like where we are. She sent him an image of her leopard disdainfully shaking its paws. *I'm not much of a swimmer.*

Your leopard is as black as Sunscar's skin!

Chantal was flattered by the surprised delight behind his

words. *Yep. Comes in handy for conducting surveillance on the graveyard shift. Not even the ghosts can see me.*

Statue stomps became statue splashes, punctuated by unintelligible shouting from the fairies.

Nibi shared what she was seeing. The short, fanged cherub statue walked into the water as ordered and got stuck on the bottom of the river. The tall, hunchback forest-giant statue ignored the shouting fairies and went after its companion.

The fairies yelled at the statues, at the castle, at their misbegotten aunt, and each other. They nearly came to blows by the time the forest giant reappeared on the river bank carrying the muddy cherub.

Finally, it occurred to Trixis to use the orange crystal geas wand from the box they'd brought. Omorachi unlocked the chain and harness, and Trixis compelled Nibi to follow them along the walkway, down the stairs to the riverbank, and up toward the castle.

Everyone in Sunscar's telepathic network felt both Nibi's anger at being compelled and her joy and relief at being free of the deadly Alfar metal and the spells it carried.

If you have the chance to escape the demesne, do it, said Dauro. *You can go for help.*

No. All together is our best shot, declared Nibi. *I'll play the docile dimwit like you did and learn what I can.*

Dauro lifted his upper forepaw, which was Chantal's signal to stand up and step away from him.

Her inner leopard, suddenly reluctant to leave his embrace, slowed her movements. *He's warm and smells nice. Let's keep him.*

Chantal had a sudden, soul-deep hunch as to why her leopard had become so possessive. Despite not being able to smell his full scent and not seeing any free-floating shifter-mate magic threads, there was a fifty-fifty chance that Dauro might be her mate.

In the history of wrong-place-wrong-time meetings, this had to rank in the top ten.

Mine, pronounced her leopard. Chantal shook her head. *He doesn't want to be kept. He wants freedom, and I aim to give it to him.*

7

Dauro couldn't make himself slide into the water, even though the pretend sun was too hot and bright, and his dense bulk too heavy to lie comfortably on the sandy bank. Chantal riveted his attention as if she'd used the geas wand on him.

Sure, she was beautiful with brown skin and eyes, sensuous lips, and black hair fraying out of a braid. And sure, she was the first human-shaped female he'd seen or touched in centuries, but it was more than that. Her fierce determination to help total strangers—his friends—resonated deep in his heart. Maybe it was true what old Nessireth said, that Ice Age shifters couldn't have mates, but he wanted to spend time with Chantal.

Dauro, said Sunscar, *only you can hear this. Quit moon-gazing over the leopard woman and come back to us. She's safe for now on the bank with Rosinette's spell hiding her. Time to plan the escape.*

Sunscar was right. Dauro forced himself up onto his paws and into the water.

The river felt diminished without Nibi's presence. He'd

never realized how strong her magic was until it was absent. The same way his chest felt hollow without Chantal snuggled against him.

He drew a big breath, then descended to where the others waited for him.

Rosinette flexed her wings, sending a new stream of blood in the water. *How does Nessireth's portal pearl work?*

A spell and demesne magic, he replied. *I heard it often enough that I memorized the spell phonetically. Chantal can work the magic.*

I'll do my best, said Chantal, *but we need a fallback–*

Nibi interrupted. *Sunscar, block me. They're using the–AAH!*

Her thoughts cut off, but not before everyone felt the excruciating start of her forced shift.

We must escape. Dauro redirected the energy of his anger toward his purpose. *With the portal pearl and Chantal, we have demesne magic and a real-world guide. We have problems to solve. How do we rescue Nibi and keep her unchained? How do we free Rosinette? How do we stop the statues from recapturing us?*

Rayapkhal bared his teeth. *How do we hide what we're doing from the fairies?*

Sunscar twisted in the water. *And how do we get Nessireth's clusterfucking book?* His fins fluttered in agitation. *Nibi is hurting, but awake. I'll reconnect her to our web in a minute or two.*

Can someone show me the lock on Rosinette's chains? Chantal asked.

Sunscar arrowed through the water to hover above Rosinette's bleeding wings. He sent a detailed mental image to them all.

Is that rusting iron? No magic? she asked.

Yes, replied Rosinette. *I'm immune to burns from the Alfar* metal in the rods, but iron poisons me. *Nessireth reminded me every time she replaced the lock.*

Dauro knew about the lock and kicked himself for not realizing what the no-magic iron key he'd seen in the castle might be for.

I can probably open it, said Chantal. *I have a universal key.*

More secrets! Sunscar's rage swamped the telepathic network a moment. *Why didn't you tell us!*

Dauro was used to Sunscar's volatile nature, but Chantal wasn't. *Please forgive him. Wraiths only know fear and rage.*

Bullshit. Chantal's acerbic tone took everyone by surprise. *Wraiths can learn to project anything they want. Negative emotions just come more easily. Humans are suckers for them.*

Sunscar sent a terrifying image of himself with eyes burning and tattoos blazing, mouth open to an inhaled column of gray fog. *I eat fear to live.*

Chantal sent them all an image of a laughing wraith kissing a smiling Asian woman. *Yeah, well, you can live on love and happiness and laughter, too. Quit being a drama queen and help figure out how to get me and my key where we need to be.*

Dauro projected his thoughts hurriedly, before Sunscar could take offense and continue the argument. *Once the lock is gone, I can use my magic to push the rods out without touching the Alfar.*

Rosinette pushed off from the river bottom. *Walk along the bank under the bridge. I'll drag myself up to the water's edge.*

No, you're too big. The bank is too shallow for you to climb with hobbled wings, said Yipkash as she and Rayapkhal untwined their tails. *Rayapkhal and I will create a waterspout to lift you up to the walkway.*

I'm immune to Alfar, too, said Sunscar grudgingly. *Give me the key and I'll unlock her.*

Nice idea, said Chantal, *but the key only works for me. Can't have prisoners freeing themselves willy nilly. The under-bridge walkway has stairs on this side, too. Should I go up there like the fairies did, or stay down on the bank?*

Prisoners? Sunscar asked suspiciously.

Dauro wanted to bite Sunscar. *Quit being a thorn in the paw. She's helping!*

Unexpectedly, Chantal sent her amusement. *It's okay. I'm a deputy sheriff from Kotoyeesinay, Wyoming. It's a sanctuary town with every species you can imagine. Even formerly grumpy wraiths. We have the usual number of troublemakers to take into custody.*

Go to the middle, above where the water is deepest, said Rayapkhal.

What's Alfar? asked Kelvin.

Dauro eased closer to the young hippo. *Metal forged by dark elves and designed to hold spells and magical energy. Nessireth said it burns shifters.*

Sunscar made a rude noise in their minds. *That's because she paid to add that property, so we couldn't help each other. Like anything else, Alfar can be used for good or ill.*

The underwater current began to curve and speed up, likely the capricorns' doing. Rosinette swam into the turbulence.

Dauro nudged Kelvin. *Let's go up for air and watch.*

Just as they surfaced, Sunscar burst out of the water, transforming from white eel to glowing black wraith in the blink of an eye. Dauro had to admit that Chantal's novel "drama queen" description fit his friend perfectly.

Sunscar beckoned to Chantal, who was already on the walkway. "Over here." He sent a mental picture to show the capricorns where to lift.

Rosinette's head appeared first, then her hobbled wings and spine where the rusting lock lay against her dull charcoal-colored hide. The waterspout bobbled her considerable mass like a pebble in a fountain. It made Dauro glad he'd never annoyed the capricorns.

Chantal pulled something small out of her upper chest pocket. Toeing the raised edge of the walkway, she leaned out and down toward the water as far as she could. Unfortunately, her arm was several feet too short to reach the lock on Rosinette.

Sunscar floated closer. "I can lift you."

Chantal gave him an assessing look, then nodded. "Deal. Can you hold me like this?" She sent a mental picture.

"Yes," said Sunscar.

He landed on the walkway, wrapped his arms around her waist, then lifted up and tilted her forward slowly, until they were parallel with the water's surface.

Dauro found himself holding his breath when Chantal stretched her arm out. She missed the first two attempts to hit the lock.

The third time, she connected and turned. The hasp gaped open, but the four Alfar chains stubbornly clung to it.

Hurry, urged the Rayapkhal. *She's heavy.*

Chantal quickly put the key in her teeth, then grabbed the chains one by one to pull them off, grunting with each one. Her pain echoed across their telepathic web.

The moment the chains dropped, the waterspout collapsed. Rosinette sank.

Trusting that Sunscar would get Chantal to safety, Dauro drew a great breath, then plunged down after Rosinette.

The wyvern, rods still impaling her winds, landed on top of the chains, the lock still dangling from one of them.

This is going to hurt, Dauro warned.

Do it! ordered Rosinette.

He shut down his awareness of everything and focused

his will. The rods were bigger than anything he'd ever moved with his magic.

The rods moved slowly at first, then faster. When Dauro finally pulled them out of both wings, Rosinette screamed her pain.

Not just in her mind, but though the water, the first sound he'd ever heard from her. She screamed even louder as she struggled to unfurl her wings.

One finally stretched fully, still torn and bleeding. The other was folded in on itself and wouldn't budge.

Kelvin, said Dauro. *Go see if you can nudge her wing out.*

Me? Surprise colored his words.

Yes. You're the gentlest. The rest of us have hooves, claws, or teeth that would hurt her worse. The boy needed to quit thinking he was useless.

Kelvin grabbed a big gulp of air and dove down to where Rosinette lay moaning. He bumped her folded wing with his big round nose. The wing moved a little. A second nudge freed the spur of bone that had been caught. He swam out of the way just in time to avoid being hit by the wing as it snapped open.

Good job, praised Yipkash.

Everyone felt Kelvin's pride in his success.

Rosinette, said Chantal, *I know a kick-ass healing spell. It packs a wicked punch, but it's good.*

Sunscar dropped into the water and became an eel. *You should use it for the burns on your hands. He* swam down toward Rosinette.

The wyvern's thoughts sounded distant. *I must sleep to heal.* Her head dropped to the silt, followed by her wings. She looked like a giant alien butterfly decorating the riverbed.

Maybe it was wishful thinking, but Dauro thought

Rosinette's color looked more vibrant than it had just a few minutes ago.

Sunscar opened his wide, circular mouth and scooped up the corroded iron lock, pulling it off the chain. *This is tainting the water.* He spiraled up in the water, gaining speed, then breached the surface. When he splashed back down into the water, the lock was gone.

Nice distance, said Chantal. *Who knew eels could spit?* She shared an image of the lock resting at the edge of the sand and the grassy bank on the far side of the castle.

Clusterfuck! Sunscar swam in a furious circle. *Nibi says the fairies are expecting a team of shifter wranglers with cages to capture and transport us to a broker.*

When? asked Chantal.

Dauro shared the memory of what the fairies had said about brokers and wranglers, and gathering the collection in one place for them.

We could wait until they put us together, said Yipkash, *then pool our resources.*

I don't know your demesne, said Chantal, *but I know wranglers. Busted a big Las Vegas outfit last year. They'll be expecting trouble. Better to get out before they get here.*

She's right, said Sunscar. *The escape has to be now, while it's just two drunk fairies bumbling around.*

They're drunk? asked Dauro.

Sunscar sent an image from Nibi of two fairies at a long table, pointing wands at each other and laughing. *She says they're in the "everything's funny" stage.*

I have a crazy idea, said Chantal slowly. *Risky as hell, but here goes. I present myself at the castle door and tell the fairies I'm the advance team for the wranglers. I'm dressed for the part. When I go to check the collection, I offer to take Nibi to the staging area I've already chosen, the far side of the bridge. I cast a spell or two to keep the fairies occupied. As soon as we're over the bridge, we use my pink crystal and Dauro's portal pearl to get out. On Vieques, which is a small Caribbean island near Puerto Rico, by the way, we run for the shore, where there's a big wide ocean for you all to hide in. We know the castle statues can't handle deep water.*

If you fail, the fairies will kill you, warned Sunscar. *Or worse, sell you.*

Nibi joined the conversation. *I think it's worth a try. I can help distract the fairies.* Her mental voice sounded tired and irritable.

Dauro saw too many holes, too many things that could go wrong, but... *We've put off our escape until it's almost too late. It's now or never. Boldness and surprise are our strongest weapons.*

If you open the portal in the water right under the bridge, said Yipkash, *it will hide our escape. Rayapkhal and I can control the water long enough to keep it from flooding out.*

I can help with that, too, added Nibi, *if I shift back into my Mishipeshu form.*

Sunscar hovered almost still in the current. *We'll have to tell Rosinette.*

Dauro glanced down at her recumbent form. *Let her sleep as long as possible. In the meantime, please help me share my memories of the demesne and the castle with Chantal, so her ignorance won't doom her.*

You really can do teaching transfer? asked Chantal. *I'm impressed. That's master-level wraith talent.* Admiration rang in her thoughts. *Could you also transfer my knowledge of Vieques to you and Dauro? If something happens to me, someone else should know what to do.*

Sunscar's body twisted. *I can only do it with fear.* It was the first time Dauro had ever known his friend to be embarrassed.

Yeah, I figured. She sent a mental shrug. *I'll deal. If Dauro is up for it.*

Yes, he replied, *I will also deal.*

Every bone and muscle still ached, and he didn't look forward to the headache, but he'd be lying if he said he wasn't looking forward to connecting with Chantal. She intrigued him no end.

Sharing thoughts was usually the last step in the mating dance, not the overture, but when had he and his Ice Age sloth ever followed convention?

8

Chantal resisted the urge to shake her head again. It hadn't helped the first three times. Memories tumbled in her mind like an excited pack of wolf pups. The magic-rich demesne, the sentient castle, the shapes and power of water, the pleasure of naps, nasty fairies, beautiful friends.

She'd never expected to know what it was like to see shades of blue and green she never knew existed, or to be tall enough to touch long claws to the top of a tree.

Dominating all the memories was magnificent, tortured, generous, compassionate, lonely Dauro.

The leopard part of her was confused. How could he be their mate when there was no scent to inhale, yet how could he not, with a heart as big as a mountain and shifter magic everywhere they looked?

The human part of her knew that nothing in life, especially mating, could ever be a simple equation. The gift of telepathy between true mates was not always possible, and certainly not on the first date. Their free magic was surprisingly compatible, but shifter magic wasn't the same as shifter-*mate* magic. Untethered fairy-demesne magic distorted everything.

She was more determined than ever to get everyone out of the dying demesne. Once they were both free in the real world, she and Dauro could see if their destinies were just momentarily tangled or truly intertwined.

But for now, she had to get her aching head in the game. Once again, she was kicking herself for not eating breakfast, and tried not to think about bacon. And the fact that sooner rather than later, she needed to pee.

A quick assessment of her clothes made her glad she'd worn her sturdiest mountain-hiking gear that morning, despite the heat. The equipment belt fit right in. Her collapsible sun visor had the Kotoyeesinay town logo, but it completed the look. Somewhere, she'd lost the tie for her braid, but it wasn't coming apart too badly yet.

Calling up the memory of the shifter hunters from Las Vegas, she added a confident swagger to her walk as she approached the open castle doors.

"Hello!" she called. "It's Kitty Breton from Hunter International. I'm here to prep for the pickup."

After a long moment, Chantal heard that high-pitched voice with a now-slurred British accent. Omorachi, she now knew. "Trixis, you left th' demesne door open again."

"Did not," came a lower-pitched female voice. Trixis.

Omorachi shouted, "You're early. Come back tomorrow."

The two fairies stumbled into view, looking exactly as Dauro and Nibi had pictured them in her mind. Omorachi carried a large goblet shaped like a trumpet vine's flower.

Chantal pulled a tiny notebook and pen from her pocket. "It's today in the real world, but you're the customer. It'll be an extra late fee." She slowly opened the notebook to a blank page and started to write.

Trixis stared blearily. "How'dja find the portal without chiming in first?"

Chantal shrugged. "Instructions on file. We've done business here before. You're Trixis and Omorachi, right?" Tilting her head, she peered into the darkened entryway behind them. "Where's Nessireth?"

Omorachi giggled. "Dead!"

Trixis elbowed her hard enough to knock her off balance. "She means dead *tired*. We're her nieces, come to help her and fix up the place."

Chantal lifted her pen. "What time tomorrow?"

"Late." Omorachi giggled again. "Like old Nessie is... always is."

Trixis frowned. "How much extra?"

Dauro whispered in her mind. Ever since the teaching transfer, her connection with him was as easy as breathing.

"Two certified Alfar ingots per day," said Chantal firmly. "Any later than tomorrow, we'll have to reschedule for at least two weeks out. Half up front."

Trixis's frown deepened.

Omorachi twirled, pulling at the fluttering flare of her black-net flounce to encourage it to fly. "Oh, let her stay and finish. Elsewise, you'll forever be whining about the cost."

Trixis tossed her head, sending her pale hair flying. "Fine. We'll get the book and show you where the animals are."

"No need. I already know." Chantal shrugged. "I checked them out on my way in, but we can go again if you want." She flipped back a page in her notebook to look at her cryptic version of a grocery list. "Except the water cougar wasn't under the bridge. You already sold her? Too bad. You didn't hear it from me, but mythicals are bringing high bids right now."

Avarice gleamed in Trixis's eyes. "We still have her." Her

thumb pointed over her shoulder. "Come inside. We'll show you."

Trixis grabbed Omorachi's upper arm with sharp claws and yanked to make her follow. The other fairy all but growled when a few drops of liquid splashed out of the goblet.

Dauro's words insinuated into her mind. *Nibi says make them change her while she's still in the hall.*

Chantal put the notebook and pen back in her pocket as she followed the fairies into the castle.

The walls looked like roughly cleaved slabs, but natural quartz didn't curve into a perfect archway. None of her new friends knew what unique powers rock fairies had, but Nessireth had evidently possessed demesne magic in spades.

The entryway opened into a large, chilly grand hall that looked like it had been ransacked. Untethered glow lights floated randomly throughout, casting moving shadows as they drifted. Empty cabinets and display cases gaped open. Old tapestries lay crumpled on the floor. The few pictures still on the walls hung askew.

To Chantal's left, the table full of magical clutter that Dauro had described stood in a brighter pool of overhead mage light. To her right, about thirty feet away and facing the table, a small, brown-skinned woman with strong Native American features huddled in a low padded chair. She trembled under an old plaid blanket. Her dull expression didn't change when the fairies pointed at her.

"There she is," said Omorachi. "Better stay upwind of her, though." She leaned in toward Chantal conspiratorially and pinched her nose. "Right rank, she is."

Chantal made a dismissive sound. "We don't deal in humans." She allowed her eyebrows to rise in question. "Unless she's got shifter-mate potential?"

Trixis shook her head. "No, that's the cougar. You'll see." She crossed to the table and picked up a slender crystal wand to point at Nibi. Bending over an oversized book on the table, she flipped to a bookmarked page and spoke the words of a spell in a language Chantal didn't recognize.

She felt the raw power, though. It took all she had to hang on to her human skin. Dauro's words in her mind urging her to stay with him distracted her leopard long enough for the power to dissipate. She sent him grateful thanks.

Nibi's scream of pain transitioned into an unhappy feline yowl as she morphed into a large cougar with copper-colored scales and webbed toes. The change only took seconds and left her panting on the floor. Shifter magic and something more eldritch blew through the room in gusts.

Chantal pasted a grin on her face, glad the room was shadowed enough to hide her lying eyes. "Oh, yeah, now we're talking."

Get both fairies to drink more dew, said Dauro.

"Er," said Chantal. "I'm not supposed to talk prices, but I think you're going to have a fantastic sale." She gestured toward the half-empty bee-shaped crystal decanter on the table with glowing chartreuse contents. "If it was me, I'd be toasting with the good stuff to celebrate."

Omorachi twirled toward the table, holding up her goblet. "More!"

Trixis absently sidestepped left to grab the decanter and pour a splash on the proffered goblet. Omorachi slammed it back like she was in a contest.

Instead of pouring for herself, Trixis paused, expression distant, then put the decanter back down.

Chantal cast about for inspiration on how to get the damn rock fairy to drink the damn dew.

She's greedy, suggested Dauro.

Chantal took a half step toward the table. "Mind if I try a sip before it's gone? Nessireth's dew collection is legendary." She let some of her leopard's sly possessiveness show in her smile.

Trixis's grip tightened. "No, we don't have any extra." With a defiant glare, she took a long draught straight from the decanter.

The eldritch magic flared again. This time, Chantal knew it came from Nibi.

The fairies suddenly wilted like spent flowers. Omorachi ended up in a heap on the floor, arms spread in a perfect ballerina circle. Trixis lay across the table like a doll, half on and half off, face flat on the table, her nose inches from the corner of the book.

Keeping her eye on the fairies, Chantal edged toward Nibi and spoke quietly. "Impressive. Can you walk?"

Nibi rose to her feet, tail swishing. Her eyes gleamed bright gold-flecked green as she began padding toward the wide doorway out.

Book, reminded Dauro. *And find the bracelet that looks like a kraken.*

Chantal glided to the table. As she eased the big, thick book away from the snoozing fairy, she realized it was too big to fit inside her shirt, so she'd have to carry it. She wanted to smash the force-shift wand, but didn't dare, in case the magic explosion woke the fairies.

Tension tightened her shoulders as she scanned the hodge-podge collection on the table, feeling time slipping away. At last, she found the kraken bracelet and slipped it onto her wrist. On impulse, she stuffed several smaller charms into the bellows pocket of her pants, then scooped up the book and strode toward the exit.

The closer she got, the warmer the book became. Anti-theft spell, maybe?

Stop, Sunscar ordered. *Speak these sounds exactly.*

She halted before the threshold and whispered each syllable. The book cooled at once. She launched into a jog to catch up to Nibi-the-cougar. Demesne magic greeted her as soon as she was outside, inviting her to play.

Dauro, said Chantal, *the water will ruin the book. Is that what you want?*

After a long moment, Dauro replied. *The capricorns say it's waterproof. Nessireth brought it with her when she visited their submerged grotto.*

Was she waterproof? asked Chantal.

No more than you are. That's what the bracelet is for. Rosinette knows the spell.

She's awake, then?

We had to. Dauro answered her next question before she asked. *Her wings are mending, but weak. She's beautiful.*

Chantal smiled at the loving regard he had for his friend. She was glad he'd chosen what her aunt called the open-heart path instead of building high walls and closing himself off. Just last week, she'd been complaining about missing her friends for a few months. Four hundred years would be an unbearably long time to be cold and lonely.

Ahead, Nibi veered from the bridge path and headed toward the river bank. The water seemed to rise to embrace her as she gracefully leapt in and vanished without a splash.

Chantal clutched the book to her chest and stood at the edge. Suddenly, the kraken bracelet flared to life.

Come on in, said Dauro. *Rosinette triggered the spell.*

Cautiously, she stepped into the water. A thin, elastic bubble formed around her legs as she waded in, keeping her dry. Right before her head went under, she took a deep breath, then ducked under.

The pygmy hippo swam by, wiggling his tail, making her smile.

Follow Kelvin, said Dauro. *And no need to hold your breath.*

Instinct said otherwise, but she made herself let go of her air and breathe in. Luckily, the charm did its job. Good thing, too, because her next step took her over the silty bank edge and into the flow.

The river was much deeper and darker than she'd imagined. She could almost see the demesne magic in the water, dancing on the outside of her bubble, parting for her like tiny schools of curious fish.

The current was stronger than she'd imagined, too. She kicked with her feet and freed one hand to help herself stay on course behind Kelvin. It was sort of like the slow-motion version of riding a bicycle down a steep hill on a windy day, with only her forward momentum to keep her from being blown away.

A flash of bone-white startled her. It took her a couple of glances to realize it was Sunscar's albino eel form, spiraling around her. He was wider than her thigh and longer than she was tall.

Sorry we're scaring you, said Dauro. He sent comforting thoughts her way.

She wanted to deny the fear, but Dauro already knew. *I'm a bad swimmer.*

You're not a... Dauro trailed off. A flash of anger came from him. *Oh, I see. Those kids nearly drowned you.*

Sunscar had warned them about stray memories.

Sorry you had to get that one. She'd almost forgotten it. *They didn't mean to.*

I'll go swimming with you next time, offered Kelvin. *They won't bother you again. I bite hard.*

Thanks. His protectiveness touched her. *They're all grown now.*

The shadow below her that grew as she swam deeper

turned out to be Dauro. He looked serene and graceful as he glided through the water.

Below him, a brilliant flash of red-orange and black resolved into the outstretched wings of a sea wyvern the color of a fire opal.

Rosinette, said Chantal, trusting that Sunscar's net was still open, *you are even more beautiful than Dauro said.*

Her telepathic reply also came as soft echoes of wyvern music to Chantal's human ears. *"You are kind to say so."*

Swim to that stone footing, said Dauro, *and pick up our treasures.* He sent her an image of a woven sea-grass bag. *You'll have to hold the pearl and speak the spell.*

What footing? asked Chantal. *I only see Rosinette because she glows.*

I'll show you, said Sunscar, *but don't touch me.*

A bright curving ribbon of eel-shaped illuminated the watery depths.

Suddenly she could see Dauro's greenish-brown fur, Nibi's dark coppery form, and the pale capricorns, tails linked.

Kelvin suddenly shot upward from the riverbed toward the surface. Dauro angled up after him.

He's afraid of me, said Sunscar, regret coloring his thoughts.

Chantal sent sympathy. *Law enforcement officers get that a lot, too. It's tough to be hated on instinct, especially when you're helping.*

The stone footing belled out to a wide, rimmed ledge before plunging into the riverbed. She swam to it, then managed to get her feet on the ledge and hook one boot toe into a crevice. Luckily, the bubble seemed very flexible. Someone had helpfully carved ridges she could grab on to for stability.

That was me, said Nibi with amusement. *It's my scratching post.*

Chantal laughed as she crouched to find the flat, pillow-like bag on the ledge, stuck in a splat of sticky mud. Prying it loose with the bubble between her and the bag was even less fun than wearing welding gloves to pick up a paperclip. She decided not to ask what had been used for glue.

Her world plunged into darkness.

Sorry, said Sunscar. *I can't generate the charge any longer.*

Thank you, replied Chantal. *It's a clever way to use your eel's electricity.*

Rosinette's voice sounded stronger as she spoke in the watery music. "I'm sending lights."

A stream of will-o-the-wisps arose and swarmed around Chantal's ledge like giant fireflies.

When she looked down, she noticed that her personal air bubble was slowly enveloping the wet bag, bringing it into her space. The subtle pulse of various magics in the bag strengthened once the bubble fully surrounded it.

She rested the book on her thighs, then gently pried open the bag's loosely sewn top and pulled out the small gray pearl.

She nearly dropped it when the magic sparked and spoke.

"Where would you like to go today, Brightest Star Rock Ruler Nessireth Amethyst Dolomite Felgranum, Owner of the Best Collections Ever?" The voice was loud, low, and gravely, like the sound of crushing rocks formed into words.

Magic pressure rose. She sent a slightly panicked thought to Dauro. *I need the portal pearl spell now while this thing still thinks I'm the former owner.*

"Er, do you have a name?" It wasn't what she'd planned

to ask, but it felt right. She yawned against the rising pressure.

The voice finally answered. "I am Pearl of the demesne."

In her mind, Rosinette spoke the words slowly, with a layer of music that wormed into her brain. She repeated them aloud just as slowly and carefully. Because it felt right, she used demesne magic to shape the words as keys as she spoke.

Sweat dripped down her neck. The unabated pressure of magic hurt her head as the voice spoke. "You are not Nessireth."

Chantal gulped. "No. I'm a guest who accepted the gift of the pearl. Is that a problem?"

After five of the longest seconds of her life, the voice spoke.

"No."

The magic pressure dropped precipitously, making her feel almost dizzy with relief.

"Where would you like to go today, Speak Your Name Here?"

Her very magical mother often said charms occasionally needed rebooting, just like mundane computers. Somehow, they must have met the magical requirements of the charm and caused it to reset.

"What are my choices?"

It wasn't safe to keep holding the tiny pearl, but it probably required skin contact. After a few seconds of thought, she opened her shirt and pushed the pearl into her camisole and bra, under her breast. It only felt odd for a moment.

"Castle cellar. Magic vault. Studio. Six habitats. Trade door. Four anchors." After a pause, it added, "Only the central anchor is available at this time."

Dauro, are you and the others hearing this?

Yes, he replied. *Yipkash says the anchor. That's where you first met them.*

"Pearl, please open a large portal to the central anchor point at ground level." She focused her will to envision an entry big enough to fit a giant aquatic sloth and a sea wyvern.

Nothing happened.

Chantal, said Dauro, *tell it where to start the portal.*

Clearly, she shouldn't have overslept so often for Beginning Fairy Portals class.

"Pearl, please set the opening in the water under the bridge."

"As you command."

Demesne magic deafened her magical senses. The free-floating strands in the water became orderly arrows, heading toward a tiny point of light centered below her. Rosinette pushed away hastily with a musical yelp as the light became an expanding gold ring.

Water roiled, creating chaotic waves that sent Sunscar tumbling until he swam out of it.

Currents buffeted Chantal as she clutched the bag and book tightly with one arm and clung to the pillar ridge.

The pearl's voice rumbled in her ear. "Portable portal paused until trade-door portal stabilizes."

"What?"

We're clusterfucked! snarled Sunscar in their minds. *That's what the castle statues use.*

No, said Nibi, *they have their own near the tall trees.*

Chantal, said Rosinette, *ask the demesne.*

Okay. Except she didn't know how to get its attention, much less talk to it.

As she shoved the wet treasure bag into her shirt with the pink crystal, she thought back to when the demesne had wanted to help her heal Kelvin. Like it was looking for something to do.

Taking a deep breath, she let it out slowly and fired up a little of her free magic to create the faint illusion of a security monitor, like human-world guards used. She imagined it showed a glowing door.

Demesne magic swirled around and through her bubble in whorls, then solidified the image, morphing the door into a wide, warehouse-style door, and adding detail to the surrounding area. From stray memories that weren't hers, she recognized Rosinette's grove.

She shaped words as magic. *Who is behind the door?*

The solid door became transparent, revealing a man and a woman, with overlays of hyena heads, suggesting they were shifters. Between them, a human woman held up a wand in one hand and a glowing charm in the other. Behind them loomed three massive trucks, each laden with two giant cages each. A fourth truck held more shifters of various species and tanks with two creatures that looked like giant sea urchins with starfish arms and legs, and glowing gems above their multiple eyes.

Shifter wranglers.

Can you delay them? she asked.

Demesne magic swirled in turbulent consternation.

Dauro's memories reminded her that the drunken fairies had ordered the demesne to let the wranglers in and be nice.

Hastily, she changed her illusion to show a wide, flat road that would support the trucks. *This would be a nice gesture,* she suggested, *so they can travel comfortably.*

Demesne magic danced, played on her bubble again, then vanished.

It's the hunters, she told Dauro and the others. *I may have* talked the demesne into sending them the long way around the far perimeter.

Sunscar swam upward fast. *I will track them. Go without me if the portal opens before I get back.*

Chantal felt a wave of sadness from Dauro, and sent him sympathy and a wordless query.

I'm afraid he means to sacrifice himself to save us. It's what he thinks he was made for.

The portal pearl's rocky voice spoke. "Portal commencing."

An unexpected underwater jet ripped Chantal from her ledge. Frantically tightening her hold on the book, she tried to kick with her feet, but the current ignored her feeble efforts. Mage lights trailed after her, trying to keep up.

The currents began to curve into a visible whirlpool, transforming into the gold-colored rings of a portal. Her shoulder slammed hard into another bridge footing, threatening to loosen her hold on the book.

Help, she sent. *I need to be at the portal's edge so my crystal fools the unauthorized passage defenses.*

On my way, replied Dauro. *Kelvin, go to the capricorns. Nibi and Rosinette, join them when you can.*

The next moment, Chantal found herself wrapped in a paw and pressed on her side against Dauro's chest. She curled her legs up to help cradle the book. His long claws extended past his shoulder. She didn't mind when coarse strands of his thick fur infiltrated her personal bubble to tickle her ear. For the first time since entering the water, she felt safe.

Pressure from the forming portal pushed her magical senses into overdrive. The pink crystal inside her shirt got warmer the closer Dauro got to the still-growing gold rings of light.

It's nothing I can explain, she told them all, *and I don't know how, but I think we all need to go through at the same time.*

Leave that to us, said Nibi. *Work your magic.*

The color of the water began to change as it swirled over and around the portal. Bright yellow rays of sunlight lit up the whole underwater portion of the bridge. The collection of captives stood poised on the river bottom, focused on the ring.

The portal solidified. A rush of water bowed into the opening like a balloon filling.

Now! ordered Nibi.

Dauro swam forward.

Close your eyes when you go through, Chantal warned him, worried the tropical sun would hurt his dark-adapted eyes.

The crystal seared her stomach. Frantically, she asked the demesne magic to help her and her friends through the portal, then close it behind them. And because it seemed like the right thing to do, she promised she'd come back to play soon.

Everything stilled for a long moment, and then she and Dauro fell in a tumble of air and water toward a wide pool of rainbow-colored fairy magic.

Frantically calling her own magic, she asked the pool to give her friends the softest landing possible.

9

D auro clung to the treasure in his paws and dropped through the portal.

Unfamiliar heat and very familiar pain wracked him. He was being force-shifted to human as he fell.

To his deep shame, he couldn't hang on to Chantal as his body remade itself. With the ground rushing toward him, he regretted not telling her that he loved her. Once again, he'd waited until too late to say important things.

Instead of smashing into the oddly colored water with a bone-shattering impact, it felt like sinking into a lake-sized pillow. Inexplicably, he now faced up, dizzily looking at the tops of trees and puffy white clouds in a brilliant blue sky.

In that instant, his physical and magical senses came online and overwhelmed him.

Magic surrounded him, soothed him. The hilly land had little water. Millions of colors everywhere, and so bright that his eyes watered.

But the smells were awful. Dirt, grass, cactus, dung, fresh urine, decay, metals, salt... He was learning there were drawbacks to context memories. He tried rolling over to bury his nose, but the multicolored fluff supporting him was no help. Waves of hot and cold nausea hit hard, making him heave involuntarily.

He tried telepathy, but no one answered. He'd sometimes wished to be alone in his head, but this was exactly the wrong time.

"Chantal!" His voice sounded pathetically raspy. "Kelvin! Nibi!"

Still no answers came as he struggled to half swim, half crawl in the magical fluff.

Unmistakable retching sounds came from the right. He shifted his direction. The stench would probably kill him, but he had to help.

Dauro? Chantal's tentative voice in his mind flooded him with relief.

Chantal! Are you hurt?

No, just hungry. Or I was, until everyone started throwing up. How about you?

Miraculously well, considering the long fall into whatever this is. But the smells are overpowering.

I felt your forced shift and saw the others. I think it's magical rebound, now that you're not having to follow the demesne's rules. I know it hurt, but it's probably better not to have to explain how aquatic creatures appeared on dry land. I'll ask the pool to bring everyone to shore.

The colorful fluff became a gentle wave that pushed him backward. He maneuvered himself around until he was facing the right direction, and counted his lucky stars for Chantal's phenomenal magical gifts.

Moments later, his fingers brushed mud. Dropping to his knees, he found purchase on the ground and crawled out of the fluff and onto dirt that smelled of everything it had ever touched. He fought another heave and tried to be grateful he hadn't eaten that day.

His gaze landed on Chantal, beautiful in the full vibrant color of his human vision, still wearing her visor hat, still carrying Nessireth's book in one arm.

She smiled when she saw him and launched into a quick trot, headed his way.

"Stop." He buried his nose in the crook of his elbow. "Sorry. I can't handle any new smells right now." It would be an inauspicious first scenting if he promptly threw up on her.

She ground to a halt, frowning. "Yipkash and Rayapkhal had the same problem when I found them the first time." Suddenly she snapped her fingers. "The demesne suppressed scents. I thought I was allergic to something, but it was the demesne rules. I bet rock fairies are super-sensitive to smells, so Nessireth had the demesne nullify them."

It made sense, once he considered it. Trixis and Omorachi had complained often about how much everything stank in the dying demesne. And Nessireth wouldn't have cared what suppressing the smells did to shifters who relied on scents for social interaction. Hell, the old fairy probably considered the impairment a bonus to help keep them in line.

Chantal turned to her left, her gaze on a figure moving in the foggy fluff. "Kelvin, this way. Listen to my voice." She sidestepped that direction. "It's okay. Just lie there a minute until your stomach settles."

Dauro sat up on his heels and looked around. The uneven wind blew hot and dry. The scrubby shrubs and gnarled trees looked like they'd had a hard life.

Chantal walked farther away along the shore of whatever was in the pond. "Nibi! Rosinette! Yeah, I know, everything stinks. Sorry about the pee smell, but I had to go. If it's any consolation, leopard urine would have been a hundred times worse."

From his loose collection of stray memories, he had an equally loose idea of where they were versus where they wanted to be. As the crow flies, they were only two miles from the ocean.

Unfortunately, none of them were crows. They weren't even animals at the moment. His sloth side had submerged into a deep sleep the moment his human shape took hold. He couldn't blame it for wanting rest after four hundred years of vigilance.

Disorientation made him dizzy. His magic felt like someone else's. It might have been the real world, but nothing felt real except the obnoxious smells.

Thank the gods for the comforting spark of Chantal's presence in his mind. Not to mention, the tantalizing golden threads of shifter-mate magic he never expected to see for himself.

It was too late to pretend he wasn't profoundly affected by her. But he could put off doing something about it until they evaded the storm of trouble still hanging over their heads. Just because the portal was closed now didn't mean it would stay that way.

Chantal strode farther along the shore. "Yipkash! Rayapkhal! This way!"

He watched the couple struggle to their feet and help each other stagger toward him and the others. As humans, they were shorter and paler than he'd imagined, with black and gold in their matted hair and in Rayapkhal's rough beard.

Actually, none of his friends looked the way he'd pictured them in human form. Nibi was short and muscular, heavy-breasted and wide-hipped, with brown skin and strong features, and long, straight, but tangled black hair. Rosinette had delicate features and a lithe build, with pale white skin, and waist-length, wavy, red-blonde hair, plus noticeable silvery scars on her arms, shoulders, ribs, and back. A legacy of the iron, perhaps.

Kelvin, on the other hand, looked exactly like his picture, except he was moaning miserably instead of grinning.

Chantal whistled for attention. "I know you're all sick, but we're too vulnerable here." She pointed toward a hill. "That way is north to a road that will take us to the southeast shore. As soon as we get clear of the fairy magic's influence, I'll try the radio and ask for help."

Nibi moved her hand from her mouth long enough to ask, "Help from whom?" Her abdomen spasmed.

Dauro looked away, in case it triggered his own stomach again. Even the thought of water made his diaphragm contract in warning.

"Flamingo shifters. I came with them to help survey the damage from the storm. Assuming they're still here." She frowned. "If they aren't, we'll go with Plan B."

One of Dauro's stray gifted memories showed him busy humans unloading wood panels and tools from a corrugated metal shipping crate big enough to hold his sloth.

Chantal pointed to the sun above the tops of the trees. "Based on that and the heat, I think it's about three in the afternoon, but it's not necessarily the same day I left. Demesnes don't always track to real time."

Dauro got to his feet and stood, willing the heaving to stop. "She's right. We should leave. Let's go find the road to the ocean."

Chantal nodded, then crossed closer to Kelvin. "I'll give Dauro the book and carry you a bit, until you feel better."

Kelvin pushed himself up. "I can make it."

Dauro crossed to help him stand. "Nibi, Rosinette, you help each other, too. Together is better."

Chantal gave him a soft smile. "You're a good man." She turned and started toward the hill.

Funny how such simple words could warm him far more than the blazing sun.

The walk up the hill was an embarrassing reminder of how uncoordinated he still was as a human. And of how tender his skin had become. As a clan warrior, thick calluses had protected his feet from the hard ground and his hands from cultivating the earth or and carrying a weapon. But after four hundred years of living in the water, every twig and pebble brought blood.

The smells weren't getting any better, either. Kelvin reeked of stale odors and sour stomach acid. Whiffs of Chantal's concentrated sweat combined a spicy citrus undertone with nothing else he recognized. The others behind him retched several times. Only the pain from scratchy shrubs and the determination to match Chantal's brisk pace kept him from doing the same.

Nibi muttered a litany of inventive curses as they climbed. Yipkash and Rayapkhal spoke encouragingly to each other in their native language. They were going to make great parents.

At the top of the hill, Chantal waited to the side until they were all together. "There's the road." She tilted her head toward a smooth dirt path. "Shifters won't care that you're naked, but humans live on the island, too. If anyone acts scandalized, I'll tell them you were on a back-to-nature retreat and got lost." She glanced at Dauro's hand resting on Kelvin's shoulder. "He can be your son."

She pulled her radio out of its holster with deft fingers. "Dammit. The demesne must have drained it." Putting it away, she turned north. "There's an abandoned truck on our way up the road. If we're lucky, the truck battery can recharge it. There's a good resting spot just over that ridge."

Dauro thanked the gods for sending them a resourceful rescuer who could be a leader when needed. It didn't hurt that they were all motivated to get the hell away as fast as they could. And that they all knew they could trust her, thanks to Sunscar.

Dauro could barely help himself and Kelvin stay on their feet at the moment, but he vowed to the ancient Heart of the Sky that he would find a way to rescue his noble friend. They would have all gone feral without Sunscar to create the telepathic web to keep their human minds alert.

By the time they got to the promised resting spot, Dauro felt like he'd marched for days in the searing heat of high summer through a thicket of thorns, and Kelvin hissed in pain every other step. None of them had breath for talking, or strength for anything but sitting in the shade of the twisted tree. At least his nausea had retreated.

He did have enough energy to watch Chantal as she used a bandana to wipe sweat off her face and neck while eyeing the road ahead. Dirt streaks all over her and straw in her fraying braid spoke of a tumbled landing. The pink crystal peeked out from under the front of her partially buttoned shirt. Miraculously, she'd hung onto the book despite everything.

Her generous lips mesmerized him. Not just because they were a work of art, but because he wanted to caress hers with his and find out what she tasted like. And touch her, skin to skin...

She turned unexpectedly and caught his gaze. Her brown eyes widened and flashed gold before she looked away.

While the first flush of desire he'd felt in centuries gave him hope that he wasn't disabled for life, the timing stank worse than his armpits. Tearing a clump of grass and smelling it helped distract him, but his stomach gurgled in protest.

Chantal's gaze swept the group. "I'm sorry you're all hurting. Is there anything in the book that would help? Or maybe your treasures? I still have the bag." Reaching into her shirt pocket, she pulled out a handful of charms and showed them on her open palm. "Plus, I pilfered these from the dew-hammered fairies."

Rosinette spoke for the first time. "The ruby ring compels truth. Nessireth used it on all of us at one time or another. The small rock hammer opens her cellar. I gather her foolish nieces didn't recognize it. The cloudy-looking glass is for mirror mages. The necklace is a charm that generates clothes from plants the way elves do. Nessireth only knew it was a wyvern scale. She traded for it to taunt me after I annoyed her with another escape attempt."

"It's yours," declared Chantal. "If you can stand the smell of me, I'll put it on you right now."

Rosinette smiled. "I'll hold my breath."

Chantal stepped in and hurriedly draped the necklace over Rosinette's hair, then stepped back.

The chain sparkled and expanded as it slithered onto Rosinette's scarred shoulders. Powerful magic flared, waking his own magical senses. In a matter of moments, the area around her was scoured clean of anything organic, and she now wore flat, brown shoes and a short, green tunic.

"If it's not too much to ask, could you make shoes for the boy?" asked Rayapkhal, pointing to Kelvin's bloody feet. "He doesn't heal as fast."

Rosinette nodded. "I can make clothes for all of you, but it will be easier with living plants to work with."

Dauro frowned. "At what cost to you?" Magic was never free.

"Oh," she said with a straight face, "feed me a fairy or two, and I'll be fine."

Nibi laughed. "Oh, sister, you'll have to stand in line for that."

Rosinette smiled. "To a wyvern, magic is like breathing, even when I'm human. I thank you for your concern, Sinchi."

"If you'll hold the book," said Chantal, "I'll collect the raw materials."

At Rosinette's nod, Chantal stepped forward to hand it to her.

Dauro pushed himself to his feet and moved to the edge of the shade. "I will stand watch."

Chantal nodded and strode across the road to the ravine on the other side.

Resolutely putting his desire to follow her aside, he turned his attention to listening. He didn't hear as well on land as other shifters, but much better than humans, so hopefully, he'd hear them first.

A trilling bird song came from somewhere up the road. The first he'd heard since they arrived. Come to think of it, the first he'd heard in centuries. Nessireth had detested birds.

He vowed not to take things like that for granted ever again. He'd not only been given a second chance for living, but a first chance for a mate.

More sounds came, now that he was listening instead of feeling sorry for himself. Different birds. Insects, lizards, and small rodents, too. And of course, more nose-burning scents. Why couldn't human bodies have nose flaps, like aquatic sloths? He concentrated on learning the frequency and rhythm of the sounds, so he'd know when they changed.

Chantal finally reappeared with an impressive armful of

leafy branches and set them in front of Rosinette. "The recent hurricane shredded most of the trees and bushes around here. I can bring a lot more deadfalls, if you can use them."

"These will do." Rosinette beckoned to Kelvin. "Come, young hippo. You first."

With quick bursts of magic, they soon all wore flexible, woven foot coverings with thick soles, loose green pants with a drawstring waist and pockets, and loose green tunics with chest pockets. Clothes felt weird on his skin. If he was honest, his smooth skin felt weird, period.

For her part, Rosinette seemed energized. "We all smell terrible, but I am glad to use magic again after so long to help my friends. The clothing design is modern, from Kelvin's memories."

"How long were you captive?" asked Chantal. "If it's not impolite to ask."

"Forty-three thousand and seventy-one days. Over a century." Rosinette offered up the book to Chantal. "And thanks to you, not one day more."

Chantal shook her head. "Just doing my job. Please keep the book, if you don't mind carrying it. By rights it belongs to all of you, not me."

Rosinette nodded and hugged it to her chest. "I will keep it safe."

Chantal turned to look at them all. "My plan is still to stop at the truck long enough to charge the satellite radio, call the flamingos, and get to the ocean. Are you all okay to pick up the pace?"

When they all agreed, she strode purposefully out of the shade and started trotting, slow at first, then faster.

Dauro took up the rear as a warrior should, and because each of his legs had its own idea of how to walk. If he fell, he didn't want to take anyone else down.

It was one thing to have other people's memories of trucks, and quite another to see one up close. And smell it.

"Ugh!" Kelvin covered his mouth and nose with the hem of his tunic. "Gasoline."

"Sorry," said Chantal. "Move upwind if you can. The smell will be worse in the shade. The good news is, I think this is the same day as I left. Otherwise, the gas smell would have dissipated." She turned toward the steep ravine the vehicle seemed to be stuck in. "Cross your fingers that the battery has juice."

Dauro caught Kelvin's eye and tilted his head. "Let's go up the road." The boy still limped, but less pronounced than before. "Is that a big truck?"

"Nah." Kelvin used the hem of his tunic to wipe a sheen of sweat off his forehead as they walked. "That's just a rusty old farm truck. The really big ones are taller than your sloth and eighty feet long. They'd never fit on this road."

The terrain inclined toward a higher hill. "How's your foot?"

"Better than my stomach." He was silent for a long moment. "What's going to happen to me after this?"

Dauro stopped and put his hand on the boy's thin shoulder. "What do you want to happen?"

Kelvin's words rushed out. "I want to stay with you until I can find my aunt." His gaze dropped as he scuffed one foot. "She might still be a prisoner."

"Where are your parents?"

"They fight a lot." Kelvin's foot scuffed harder. "My aunt is looking after me because they needed space."

So many obstacles ahead. Not the least of which was his ignorance of… pretty much everything.

"You know I love you, yes?" At the boy's nod, Dauro breathed deep. "But you also know I have nothing. No clan. No home. No living family. I would be a very poor…"—he settled for the English word that came closest to the right one from his native tongue—"...guardian."

Distant thunder reached his ears.

Kelvin shaded his eyes and looked to the sky. "I hear a helicopter."

An image of a big flying machine with whirling blades popped into Dauro's head. His new context memories didn't explain how it stayed in the air.

"Hide," shouted Chantal. "They might not be friends."

Dauro pointed toward the low trees on the side of the road and crossed to force his way into the thicket. The stabby branches would have been worse without his tunic. Kelvin joined him. The close-up smells weren't quite as bad as before, giving him hope that his nose was acclimating to the real world.

The helicopter sounds grew louder. Moments later, a yellow and black helicopter flew into view and slowed.

Without warning, Dauro's magical senses lit up.

Kelvin jumped like he'd been bitten. "What was that?

"Magic locator spell." So much for hiding. Shifter magic might be bound up in the ability to shift, but it was still magic.

The helicopter continued its slow flight over the road, then picked up speed and altitude.

"It's coming back around," said Kelvin.

"Let's stay hidden. No sense giving away more information than we have to." And no sense using his own warrior magic to shield his and Kelvin's signatures, either. The runaway horses had already stolen the barn door.

The noisy helicopter flew by again, even more slowly, but no locator spell this time.

Dauro waited with Kelvin until the helicopter sounds disappeared before jogging back to join the others.

"Plan B," announced Chantal as she stood on the cab of

the truck, fists on her hips. "Free the truck and drive like a bat out of hell for the shore."

"Does it even work?" Yipkash's tone matched her skeptical expression as she eyed the metal behemoth.

"Worth a try," said Chantal. "We'll give it ten minutes, then go for Plan C."

"Which is?" asked Nibi, who was already headed toward the truck.

Chantal jumped into the truck bed. "Run like hell for the shore."

Rosinette sat on the ground. "This is my failure. I should have been hiding us all." She opened the book. "Nessireth lied all the time, but she bragged often about war spells she acquired after her ex-tribe tried to steal her demesne. I will look for them."

From experience, Dauro knew Rosinette could not be argued from her self-assumed guilt, regardless of her innocence. He caught Kelvin's eye and pointed back up the road. "You are the sentry. Howl like a wolf if you see or hear trouble."

Kelvin nodded once and turned without argument.

Dauro's respect for the boy grew. He'd make a fine warrior someday, if he wanted. Or not. Modern life held a dizzying array of opportunities.

With shifter strength fueled by desperation, they quickly freed the truck from the tangled trees and pushed it onto the road.

Dauro wanted to throw the nasty, half-empty gasoline can as far as he could, but the others wouldn't let him. If the stuff was that bad for living things and started wildfires, why did humans even use it?

He moved to stand on the road edge next to where Rosinette sat, still reading. Chantal climbed up the truck's front and stuck her head under the open hood. Nibi sat in the cab behind the wheel. At Chantal's signal, Nibi leaned forward and did something.

The shriek from the truck was worse than the new smells, which at least weren't turning his stomach anymore. He put his hands over his ears.

Chantal stood up. "Starter's half stripped. Try again."

After several squealing protests, the engine finally caught and ran on its own.

Dauro dropped his hands. He'd just have to get used to how clusterfucking cacophonous the real world was.

Chantal slammed the hood closed and jumped down. She grinned and crossed to him. "Let's rock and roll, handsome. Bring the bookish wyvern and climb on in." She wiped her smudged palm on her pants, then held her hand out to him.

His hand slipped into hers and he stepped in close before his common sense could intervene.

"You are amaz..." The first full noseful of her scent stunned him like a lightning bolt. No word in any of the languages in his head encompassed his feelings. The flush of desire. The depth of wonder. The sense of rightness, like coming home.

Her pupils dilated as her breath caught. "So are you." Her hand rose to touch his neck, then slid up to his jaw and ear. "I never dreamed–"

A loud whistle pierced his fog. Nibi waved urgently at them. "Let's go!"

Chantal cupped his face with both hands and fixed him with an intent look. "To be continued."

All he could do was nod as she let him go and stepped back.

Kelvin was climbing into the cab. Rayapkhal and Yipkash were dragging fallen branches into the truck bed for camouflage. Dauro moved to help them, but Chantal continued to command his attention.

"Rosinette." Chantal crouched in front of the sea wyvern's slender human form. "Time to go."

Rosinette blinked like she was surprised to see the world. "Sorry?"

Chantal laughed. "Bribe a shifter with food, but bribe a wyvern with a book." She stood and pointed a thumb toward the truck. "Let's go for a ride."

Rosinette closed the book and rose to her feet with smooth grace. "With pleasure."

Chantal climbed into the cab, where Nibi and Kelvin made room so she could get behind the wheel and slam the door.

Dauro didn't know about the pleasure part, because the back of the truck was loud and smelly, but he really liked the going fast part. Sloths didn't do fast.

Rosinette, seated across from him, clutched the book with eyes closed. Subtle magic from her tickled his senses.

Surprisingly, Yipkash moved to sit beside him instead of her mate. "If… no, *when* we get free and go back to Greece, Raya and I want you to know our land home is open to you for as long as you need. Once our children are born, we must live in the sea until their first shift."

In odd moments, Dauro had been worrying about his future. Yipkash's offer gave him an option he'd never imagined. "That's very generous."

"Your love for all of us made Sunscar less surly and Nessireth's heartlessness bearable. It's the least we can do." She nudged his shoulder with hers with a smirk. "It's near a resort. Bring the leopard. She likes you."

He shook his head. "I am a relic. She has a life."

Yipkash laughed. "So did I. Marine biologist. Meeting and

mating Rayapkhal changed the direction of my life's current for the better." She nudged him again. "My advice, which you didn't ask for but I'm giving anyway. Talk to her. She shepherds all of us, but her gaze starts and ends with you."

"I will." He had nothing to offer her but his heart, but it was hers for the taking.

10

Chantal gripped the steering wheel as another bottom-scraping rut sent Nibi and Kelvin bouncing into each other.

"Whoever planned these roads should be eaten for lunch," groused Nibi, rubbing the elbow she'd cracked against the passenger door's window that wouldn't roll down. The driver's side window refused to roll up.

"The former sugar factory or military engineers, take your pick." Chantal wanted to bite whoever cut the damned seatbelts off in the cab. "Kelvin, what's the battery percentage?"

A cord stretched from the cigarette lighter to the satellite radio in his hands.

"Twelve."

"Good. Try now. Put it on speaker like I showed you." She had to slow for the switchback turn Nibi had complained about, but kept her foot hovering over the accelerator. Thank the goddess for automatic transmissions.

Her focus was fraying in a hundred directions just when

she needed to concentrate. Enemies in helicopters—probably. Flamingos looking for her—maybe. A balky truck and a road trying to kill her—absolutely. A sexy, spicy man whose scent sent her spark gauge way past red—

"Kitty One to Base," said Kelvin into the radio.

"Rock!" shouted Nibi.

Chantal was already slamming on the brake and guiding the drift from the wheel. Bald tires made the fishtailing slide around the obstacle easier to achieve, but harder on her tumbling passengers. "Sorry!"

"You're a maniac!" Nibi's grin belied her complaint. "Where did you learn to drive?"

"My dad's an independent trucker. I was driving mountain roads before my first shift."

A flare of wyvern magic came from behind the cab.

Chantal narrowed her attention to the road and the map in her head. So far, they hadn't run into any other traffic, but that would change the closer they got to the beach. She could already smell the salt in the air.

A burst of static came from the radio. *"Base to Kitty One. We were about to send a team for you. It would have been sooner, but we had visitors land with three big trucks on the north shore."* Leticia's calm tone relieved one of Chantal's worries. *"You sound different, and the GPS is still wonky. Are you okay?"*

"I'm Hippo One, Kitty One's assistant," said Kelvin proudly. "She wants you to meet us at Brown Duck Beach."

Chantal accelerated on the straightest stretch of road she'd seen yet. "What visitors?"

"Wizards and shifter hunters loaded for big game. They weren't after us, so we spied on them. They opened a portal near Monte Pirata and disappeared. Shouldn't have been possible."

Chantal hunched to look under the crack in the windshield. "The portal goes to an anchored fairy demesne. We just escaped from there an hour ago."

"Who is 'we'? The two people you found?"

The truck labored noisily up the small incline. She raised her voice. "Me and six shifters who escaped from the collector's demesne."

Leticia swore a vicious oath in Spanish. *"Meaning the hunters might be after you."*

"Yeah, probably. The fairies might send giant animated stone statues, too." Chantal slowed for the blind curve and the upcoming intersection. "I think they're already looking."

More wyvern magic flared from behind her. Up front, a familiar shadow appeared on the road.

The yellow and black helicopter had found them.

Or should have. Instead, it hovered a moment then flew slowly west, away from them. She hoped it was because Rosinette's magic hid the truck and its dust cloud.

Chantal flared a little magic of her own, giving her a magical view of the topography and a sense of the safest direction to the ocean. A trick she'd learned from her mother.

"We aren't prepared for hunters, but we aren't without resources," said Leticia. *"Someone will meet you at the beach."*

"One more thing," said Chantal. "Call the Kotoyeesinay Sheriff's Department. Tell them I said we need fairy portal and demesne specialists as fast as we can get them. The demesne is dying. If it fails, it'll put Hurricane Chantal to shame."

"Will do." The call ended with another burst of static.

"The hurricane that shook the demesne was named Chantal?" Nibi made a rude sound. "The Powers are in a meddling mood."

"Oh, yeah." Her magic nudged her. She reached over her head to slap the naked metal roof twice. "Hide!" she shouted. "Traffic!"

By the time a music-blaring, garishly-painted tourist

Jeep rolled by on the paved road, Chantal was alone in the old truck loaded with deadfall branches. Just another uninteresting local with a load for the debris pile.

The second the Jeep rounded the curve, she turned right onto the asphalt, then left onto the narrow dirt road that headed south.

Picking up as much speed as she dared, she leaned in toward her seatmates to avoid branches of the high shrubs that threatened to break off the side mirror. She slapped the roof again. "Hang on!"

The road dropped down into a muddy creek bed. She tightened her grip on the steering wheel and gunned the engine, willing the truck to find traction and get them up onto the road again.

Two jaw-clenching moments later, they made it, barely, flinging mud and loose branches from their tires.

After disentangling herself from Kelvin, Nibi patted the cracked vinyl of the front console. "Good girl!"

A thought struck Chantal. "Nibi, Kelvin, can you swim shifted in salt water?"

"My aunt took me to the beach in Mexico last year," said Kelvin. "I float. Sort of."

"Never tried," said Nibi. "My sister did, though, and she's still alive. Or she was when Nessireth's hunters caught me in 1958."

"We'll find her." Chantal spared a brief glance at Kelvin. "Your aunt, too." She would make it her personal mission, if she had to. That horrid, greedy fairy had cost them so much.

Without warning, the brush cover ended. So did the road. A couple hundred feet of dark, rock-and-sand beach lay between them and the ocean.

She braked to a stop before the truck got stuck in softer sand the recent storm surges may have deposited. That was the hazard she imagined, anyway. She'd never been so close to that much water all in one place, except in the boat ride to the island. And never in a truck older than she was with bald tires and no damn seatbelts.

Nibi put fingers to her lips and whistled loud enough to make Chantal's ears ring. "Pool's open!" She piled out of the passenger door and began a quick march toward the water.

She was soon followed by Yipkash and Rayapkhal, half-trotting in almost perfect synchrony. They seemed so perfect for each other.

"Here's your radio." Kelvin held it out to her. "Can I wait to go with Dauro? He's big and strong."

Chantal couldn't disagree with that. The fairy demesne may have suppressed his magic and his sense of smell, but it hadn't prevented him from staying in shape. His muscles had muscles. "Good idea." She disconnected the cord and put it in her belt pouch, then holstered the radio.

She'd been so intent on getting the aquatic shifters to the *aqua* that she realized she didn't have a plan for herself. "Plan D."

Dauro's divine scent hit her the moment before his head appeared at her side window. "What's Plan D?" He stepped back and opened her door.

His clothes made him look like a doctor in hospital scrubs. An enticingly sexy, very lickable doctor. Her inner leopard recommended pouncing immediately, before their prize got away.

"Wait for the flamingos." She pointed toward the land finger to the east, where the beach continued. "Tell any gawking tourists not to believe their lying eyes if they think they see unusual animals in the water."

Dauro moved closer, commanding her attention, steeping her in his scent. "I will wait with you."

She inhaled slowly, savoring the uniquely mossy, earthy,

complexly minty notes that were better than anything in the world, even catnip. Hormones flooded her breasts and belly with heat. Golden threads of shifter-mate magic danced in her peripheral vision. She forced herself to look away before she did something insanely ill-timed.

"I'll wait, too." Kelvin crossed his arms stubbornly.

Rosinette's voice came from behind them in the back of the truck. "I will stay to defend you and the book."

Chantal blew out a noisy breath and caught Dauro's eye again. "I want you here more than anything. You make me feel safe. But if the statues come, Rosinette can fly out of reach, and they don't want me. Only the deep water can save you and Kelvin."

Dauro nodded. "We will swim if they come." His jaw tightened. "My sloth would shred me if I left you to face the hunters alone."

That was fair, considering that's how her leopard was feeling about him. "Okay. Plan E, it is." She turned the truck engine off.

Out on the beach, three lines of footsteps led to where Nibi and the capricorns were already knee-deep in the water, confidently moving through the waves. Yipkash and Rayapkhal dove in and vanished. Nibi pushed forward until she was chest-deep, then submerged and disappeared.

"Rosinette," said Dauro, "can you unmake the clothes you gave Nibi, Yip, and Raya? They're piled at the water's edge."

Wyvern magic flared. Not only did the clothes disintegrate into loose piles of branches, but the footprints in the sand vanished. No one hid better than wyverns.

Dauro called his thanks, then leaned his elbow on the open door's window ledge and focused on her.

Goddess, but he was sexy. Wild hair she wanted to plunge her fingers into. Smooth skinned, except for scar lines she'd seen glimpses of on his arms, now partially hidden by the tunic's short sleeves. Her skin heated.

It was hard to drag her focus back to their situation. "I'm no magical wyvern or battle mage, but I've got a few tricks up my sleeve." Chantal reached into her shirt to pull out the grass bag of treasures. "Anything in here that can help us?" She looked at Kelvin, who shrugged, then at Dauro.

He squinted one eye. "I don't know what the bracelet and the charm do. The wishbone has stolen alpha power. The chain loop dries things, but I don't know the spell."

"I do. I will teach you." Rosinette's musical voice was much easier to hear without the engine running. "Put the chain near whatever you want dried, name the target, then sing this." Wyvern magic flared. Music and words wormed into Chantal's brain like a catchy tune.

Chantal pulled the chain out of the bag and handed it to Dauro.

He wrapped it three times around his wrist. "Rosinette, you are a marvel."

"I do what I can." More wyvern magic flared. "The bracelet and charm go together. Each can be activated with a key phrase to find the other."

Chantal emptied the rest of the bag onto her lap. "Since Ice Age shifters like Dauro are immune to alphas, I'll keep the wishbone, in case the hunters try to make me submit. Kelvin, you wear the bracelet, but give Dauro the charm. That way, you can find each other if there's trouble."

Kelvin took the bracelet and opened its clasp. "What are the magic words?"

"Whatever words you say as you separate the bracelet and the charm," said Rosinette. "I suggest avoiding common phrases."

"What happens if we shift?" asked Dauro.

After a moment of silence, Rosinette answered, "The book doesn't say."

Chantal shook her head "Better assume it'll break, then. Maybe that's why Nessireth tossed it."

Kelvin frowned, then closed the clasp and gave the bracelet back to her. "I don't have a place to keep it."

Chantal nodded. "It's yours for later, then." She slid it into the zippered part of her upper chest pocket. At her inner leopard's urging, she put the empty woven grass bag in her outer pocket instead of dropping it. Her cat's instincts were more often right than not.

At the edge of her range, she heard the telltale whump-whump she'd been dreading. "Helicopter. Dauro, get in." She pointed to the passenger door. "We're just locals, avoiding the tourist beach."

The yellow and black helicopter came from around the land finger, following the shore line.

"Clusterfuck!" Rosinette's precise diction made it even more of a curse. "They're using technology I don't understand. I can't hide Nibi and the others in the water and us, too."

Chantal looked to Dauro for confirmation as he got in and slammed the door shut. He nodded.

She turned the key in the engine. "Hide the others. We just have to hang on until the flam… Oh, hell!"

A second, larger yellow and black helicopter appeared from the same direction as the first one. She pumped the accelerator, and the engine caught. "We're going back to the creek. More defensible. No place to land helicopters."

She put the truck in gear and made the reverse Y-turn slowly, fighting the urge to punch it and run. Despite her care, the truck's tires spun alarmingly before finding purchase on the harder gravel track.

The magic-locator ping came right as their front tires

hit the creek bank. She turned left into the mud and headed for an overhanging tree.

"Kelvin, pull out my radio and tell Base we've got a wizard and two yellow-jacket helicopters on our ass."

She pulled under the tree and stopped. If she left the engine running, they'd have mobility, but she didn't know how much gas they had left because the fuel-sending unit was broken. After a moment's indecision, she turned it off, but left the key in the ignition.

Kelvin made contact and told Base the bad news. Bless Leticia for her unflappable nature.

Chantal opened the door and got out, moving aside so Dauro and Kelvin could do the same. Closing her eyes a moment, she used her magic to make a detailed map of the immediate area in her head.

Chantal caught Dauro's eye. "You're the war leader. How do we act like prey, but not get eaten?"

Rosinette jumped off the back of the truck holding the book. Wyvern magic flared. The muddy area under the truck and all their feet hardened. "I will stay if you ask, Sinchi, but my only skill in battle is desperation. I propose to hide with the book and make mischief from afar."

Chantal thought Rosinette underestimated herself, but she'd let Dauro make the call.

Dauro hesitated, then nodded. "Can you also hide Kelvin? You need a sentry so you'll be free to concentrate."

"Yes." Rosinette held out her hand to Kelvin. "Your knowledge of technology will be most welcome."

Kelvin slipped his hand into hers. "Okay." He turned to look up at Dauro, worry in his eyes. "You won't leave without me?"

Dauro crouched to pull the boy in for a brief hug. "I won't leave *any* of you."

Even though the telepathic connection was closed,

Chantal melted in the wave of Dauro's abiding love for his friends. The real world needed all the open-hearted people like him it could get.

Chantal reached into the truck to grab the radio and hand it and the charge cord from her belt to Kelvin. "Call the flamingos for help."

Kelvin nodded and turned to walk with Rosinette.

Wyvern magic flared as the woman and boy walked toward the opposite side of the creek. They faded and disappeared, as if they'd never been there.

Dauro turned to her and opened his mouth to speak, but the larger helicopter flew into view and dove toward them.

She crouched next to Dauro beside the truck and covered her head against the buffeting wind from the blades.

The helicopter slowed to hover above them. A male voice boomed from a loudspeaker. "Stay still and we won't hurt you!"

It must be the tourist visor hat making her look stupid enough to believe that lie.

She'd been avoiding telepathy with Dauro because it was too tempting and distracting, but now, she had a good excuse. Touching his knee, she energized the connection and sent him her map of the area. *Around the tree and upstream through the shrubs?*

Around the tree, but downstream. The deep water is closer. Don't worry. I will swim with you.

That works. She cut off the connection fast to prevent herself from basking in the warmth of his thoughts. She couldn't afford her hormones and emotions to swamp what few working brain cells she had left. And he deserved freedom to think about what—and who—he wanted, not to be ambushed by the first leopard he'd seen in four hundred years.

Pushing off from the truck gave her enough momentum to get to the tree trunk. Dauro was right behind her.

"Fuckin–" The blaring loudspeaker cut off.

The tree's branches partially shielded them from the wind, making it easier to plunge into the dense shrubs. Her shirt's long sleeves had been making her hot and sticky ever since the escape, but she was grateful for their protection from the pointy branches. Unfortunately, her hair was catching on every one of the damn things. At least she was blazing a trail for Dauro, who only had thin hospital scrubs for cover.

The helicopter made two low passes at them. Each time, the buffeting winds slowed their forward progress, but she and Dauro still made headway.

On the third time around, the helicopter slowed up ahead. Two figures carrying heavy, modified rifles jumped out of the helicopter's open doors and cursed loudly when they landed in the brush. The helicopter rose higher and hovered.

Chantal quickly opened the connection to Dauro. *Those will be shifter-rated tranquilizer guns. I can put up a shield, but I can't do anything else magical when I do. Can't keep it up forever, either.*

Turn south, toward the cliffs.

She did at once, with him close on her heels.

It took her a few moments to realize that's what he'd planned all along. The straight path had served its purpose of luring the hunters to the ground to even the playing field.

The sounds of pursuit behind them added speed to her feet. Drawing her magical energy, she created the shield behind Dauro. She'd only have to keep it up until they reached the water.

The shrubs ended as the ground beneath her feet tilted downslope. She slowed to avoid slipping on the limestone rubble between the low-growing plants. Dauro moved to her side.

Noise arose and magic pinged them again, this time from the front instead of overhead. Damn! She'd forgotten about the second helicopter. She could almost see the pilot and passenger through the bubble canopy as the helicopter flew toward them.

A sudden cloud of pink arose from the west. At least fifty flamingos, wings wide and feet trailing, flew directly in the helicopter's path. They were taking a terrible risk, but it made the pilot send the nose up hard.

Which meant the pilot couldn't see the tentacle-shaped column of water rise from the ocean and wrap around the tail beam to drag the helicopter down. The moment the spinning top rotor hit the surface, the column disintegrated as the helicopter flipped, tumbled, and broke apart.

Crashes and curses came from behind.

The next thing Chantal knew, she was in Dauro's arms as he leapt over the cliff edge and down.

They plunged feet first into the warm blue water one moment after she remembered she didn't know how to trigger the kraken charm bracelet she still wore.

Drowning was going to be her least-favorite way to die.

This time, Dauro hung on to his treasure when the warm sea embraced them.

The moment his feet hit the murky bottom, he pushed upward with half-shifted strength borrowed from his sloth. Another long-disused skill he was having to relearn in a hurry.

He burst up through the surface and raised his treasure up higher, making sure her head was well out of the water as they gasped for air. Her hat went flying.

She pushed back and twisted in the water to look at him. "You didn't shift."

"Aquatic sloths are too big for this part of the world." He wiped water from his eyes. "Are you okay?"

"Yes, surprisingly. Let's find the deeper water before the hunters find us."

He nodded once, to honor her courage, then turned toward the horizon and started swimming. Not knowing her skills, he chose a slow and gentle frog kick. Through their link that had become stronger the moment he'd shifted to human, he knew fear nibbled at her confidence.

Her crawl stroke reminded him of his African mother, who'd taught that style of swimming to his father's clan. Surprisingly effective. Chantal pulled ahead despite being hampered by sodden clothes and heavy boots.

He'd been afraid his human body wouldn't remember how to swim, but with that, at least, he had no trouble. The lightweight tunic and pants didn't hamper his movements, and Rosinette's miraculous shoes stayed tight on his feet even when water-logged. Like everything else in the real world, the feel of water on his smooth human skin felt odd but good.

He dove under for a moment to use the more refined magic of his human side to feel for currents.

Greetings, Sinchi Dauro.

A magnificent, dark copper-scaled cougar appeared in a magical current she controlled. Her eyes glowed like emeralds.

Well met, Nibi'ikwe. I'm happy to see you. Thank you for handling the helicopter.

Our pleasure. Rosinette and the boy raised a sudden windstorm and clinging vines to disable the larger one. Her tail switched. *Unfortunately, it had already dumped two ekinos into the water, and we don't know why. Yipkash, Rayapkhal, and I are hunting them. Swim south to the tiny dry island and stay there until we give you the all-clear. I'll send you a current guide.*

Thank you. He surfaced again for air, just in time to feel the current lift and move him to Chantal's side. Too bad his human lungs weren't as big as his sloth's.

Speaking took the breath they'd need for swimming, so he energized their mental connection and told her what he'd learned.

He felt her delight and relief as she figured out how to ride the current. *It's like an underwater moving sidewalk.* She continued crawling at a slower pace, turning her head to breathe with each lift of her right arm. *What are ekinos?*

Giant spiny starfish. Nessireth got one for security. Sunscar said they came from the same laboratory where they made him. Turned out to be no brighter than a barnacle and always hungry. It would eat anything living, but preferred meat, meaning us. She finally traded it for Yipkash and Rayapkhal about twenty-five years ago.

The current curved left, putting them on course for the small island that sported a crowded clump of green trees on its rounded top. The white sand along the shore shimmered with heat.

How did you keep track of years in the demesne?

He liked that she wanted to get to know him. *I didn't, at first. In my former life, the priestesses kept the calendar and told the rest of us when to plant and harvest. The demesne had no seasons. Very confusing. When I made friends with Nessireth's other captives, I'd ask them about the real world. Sunscar helped the most by teaching me the modern calendar.*

How many captives did Nessireth have?

He deeply appreciated that none of her questions had an undertone of pity. Once their story got out, all the captives would be in for raft-loads of that. *Seven, when she acquired me. When she discovered I wasn't the elephant-seal shifter she'd been told she'd get, she traded the others for more exotics. She used me to scare anyone she invited to the demesne.*

He thought she'd laugh, but instead, she sent him a wave of sympathy. *That must have been hard.*

A century of war and invasion was hard. Boredom in the impossible river was hard. Screaming and waving my claws was easy. Her guests angered me. They were there to buy and sell, not make friends or rescue us.

She abruptly pulled her arm back and twisted away. "Something brushed... oh, it's sand."

He spiked his legs down and discovered they'd hit the shallows. "Sooner than I expected." He used his magic to test the water and the shore. "The sand is solid from here to the beach."

The current carried him a few more yards until he ran aground. After climbing to his feet, he pulled off and folded his sodden shoes and carried them. He couldn't afford to lose his only pair of shoes in the world to the sucking sand.

Chantal wrung the excess water from her loose, wavy hair as she started slogging toward the shore, high-stepping and slashing with her boots. "Come on, my handsome *sinchi.* Let's find some shade. Since we could be here a while, I'll trade you a spell to repel mosquitoes if you lend me your dryer charm."

He stayed behind a few steps, as a warrior should. And because her wet clothes revealed her strong thighs and the delicious curve of her hips as he'd never seen them before. Some of his blood supply began diverting from his brain to his groin. He imagined helping her remove the layers one by one, discovering each new part of her–

Chantal laughed. "I think you're sexy as hell, too, but we're a little busy right now."

He must have unintentionally been broadcasting again. "Sorry." Apparently, his human magic control needed practice, like everything else.

"Don't be. I would love to overshare with you, but I saw a whole pack of hunters waiting at the portal, not just the six or eight we've seen in the helicopters."

"You're right." He consoled himself with the thought that she'd called him both handsome and sexy.

Just before they got to the sunbaked sand, he stopped to put his shoes on. Chantal marched across the narrow bar of sand to the first trees, then turned and waited for him.

The broken shade wasn't noticeably cooler than the hot

sand, and forcing their way through the thick undergrowth of shrubs made for slow progress. Smells no longer nauseated him, but even though he'd vowed to be grateful for everything the free world had to offer, he'd just about had his fill of thorny branches and scratchy leaves.

She finally stopped. "Are we far enough from the shore, do you think?" Her head tilted up as she eyed a tall palm tree. "Too damn skinny to climb and check."

He sent his magic out for a quick echo. "We're just about center."

She took a deep breath and looked up toward the sky. "Your shape-of-the-land magic feels... it's very handy. Maybe I can expand my map talent to do that someday." Sweat poured down the side of her face. She wiped it away with her hand, then flicked away the excess moisture.

He unwrapped the chain from his wrist and gave it to her. "Dry yourself first. It must have been maddening to be in the water wearing all those clothes."

"Tiring, too, since I was a kitty-brain and didn't get the breathe-underwater spell from Rosinette for the kraken charm. I'd have been in serious trouble without Nibi's magic current. Not how I pictured my first ocean swim." She held up the chain. "Pants, shirt, camisole, underwear, socks, boots, and hair." She followed the words with the short song-spell Rosinette had taught them.

Sorcerer magic flared, and within moments, his hair and thin clothes were dry as a bone. He rubbed his head to get some of the caked salt out of it.

"Oops, sorry." She held out the chain to him. "I should have been more specific about *whose* things to dry."

As he took it and wrapped it around his wrist, she closed her eyes and murmured in a language he didn't know. Magic flared, then settled on his skin like an all-over caress. Of all the magic used on him in his life, hers felt the best.

Of course it does, mumbled his sleepy sloth. *She's our mate.*

"We should be invisible to mosquitoes until morning." She finger-combed her hair, then gathered and began braiding it with nimble fingers as she looked around.

He opened his mouth, then closed it again. He'd been wishing for time and privacy, just the two of them, but now, he didn't know what to say.

Being alone with her for the first time should have happened someplace special, someplace better than in the middle of an inhospitable thicket on a glorified sandbar. For once, they weren't running or swimming for their lives. Questions crowded into his head and formed a logjam at his throat.

She pulled a flexible pouch off her belt, opened its attached cap, and held it out to him. "Fresh water?"

"Yes, please." After all the salt water he'd inadvertently swallowed, the fresh water tasted cool and soothing.

"Clever device." He handed it back to her.

"My mother made it. It's always full. She's good with charms." Chantal took several gulps herself, then put the pouch back on her belt. "I'd like you to meet her and my dad." Her gaze fell away. "If you want. When you're ready."

The uncertainty behind her words worried him. "Why wouldn't I want to meet them?"

She took a deep breath, then blew it out between tightened lips. "Because I'm crowding you, worse than that fool cougar ever did me. Because we haven't talked about... anything, really. We barely know each other. Transplanted context memories don't count." She shook her head. "We did this all backwards. Telepathy isn't a bond. I'm the first free female you've scented in centuries. There are a million other shifters in the sea."

"But none of them are my mate. You are." There, he said it.

Her breath caught as she looked away. She took a deep breath, then returned her gaze to his. "My leopard says the same, and I want that. Want you. You're generous and clever. Your scent tops my spark gauge every time. Shifter-mate magic is everywhere you are."

Her expression turned troubled as she shoved her hands in her pockets. "But shifter-mate biology and magic tell us who our mates *could* be, not who they *must* be. A butthead fairy subverted your destiny for four hundred years. You and I met in extraordinary circumstances. You're still dependent on me. I'm an even worse butthead if I take advantage of that."

Her words soothed and hurt at the same time. To give himself time to think, he cleared brush from around a downed palm trunk so they could sit. Shifters had amazing strength and stamina, but they both needed time for recovery.

"Before my captivity, I spent decades becoming a strong and wily warrior so clans would want to keep me. Even in mixed clans, alphas only tolerated me because I didn't want their position. Priestesses ignored me. I had friends, but my free magic and the size of my sloth scared them. I had lovers, but we weren't mates, and no shifter female wanted to chance bearing another one of my kind." He smiled wryly. "Even with shifter senses to help with timing, our only birth control back then was luck and magic. Mostly luck."

Her fingers traced the edge of her kraken bracelet that peeked out from under her grease-stained cuff. "Modern family-planning is a great invention." The corner of her mouth twitched with humor. "But I wouldn't be here if it always worked."

He filed that tidbit away to ask her about later. "I had a lot of time in the demesne's impossible river to think about what I would do differently if I ever made it back to the real world."

She raised one eyebrow. "Never swim again?"

He smiled at her teasing. "No, the water is life for my sloth." He rubbed his jaw, where salt made his short beard itch. "For most of my life, I only noticed what I lacked, and neglected everything else to chase it. It's not the path to happiness, always wanting more. Always looking for worth from others instead of from within. I want to enjoy my bounty and live in the present." A capricious breeze shook the leaves. "But we both must take the time to be sure. You have many choices, too..."

He trailed off as a loud scraping sound caught his attention. Chantal stood and faced the still-visible path they'd created when pushing through the dense stand of trees and bushes.

"Boat?" she asked quietly as he stood.

He shook his head. "Doesn't sound right."

Glancing at the tall, skinny palm, she grimaced. "Still not climbable."

"My sloth is tall if I stand on my back legs, but I'll drain my reserves if I shift." As a warrior wanting to be valued, he wouldn't have admitted that, but he trusted Chantal.

"Better to stay human." She snorted. "We're on a tiny dry island. Your prehistoric sloth would be hard to explain."

The scraping took on a syncopated rhythm and increased in volume, then stopped. A sawing sound replaced it.

"True." As humans, they could talk their way out of being discovered.

The rhythmic scraping resumed.

She gave him a side-eyed glance. "This is going to sound paranoid, but please tell me ekinos can't survive out of water."

"They can't." He blew out a noisy breath of frustration. "But Sunscar said it takes them a while to die."

"Just great." She smoothed her hair back with both hands. "I hope it's tourists."

So did he, but he wouldn't bet his only shoes on it. They had obviously become prime entertainment for the real world's gods of mischief.

The sawing sound started again, this time deeper pitched. It was soon drowned out by the sound of something crashing through branches and leaves.

"We need intel." Chantal undid two buttons on her shirt, then pulled out the flat, thick pink crystal she'd amazingly kept safe through desperate escapes, hikes, truck rides, and a long ocean swim. "If you'll hold this for a bit, I'll go furry and scout."

The thought of being separated from her gouged a hollow in his chest, but he squelched it. She was right about needing to know what they were up against. His detection magic was only good for land and water, not living things. Except Chantal. He always knew where she was. He took the crystal.

In a matter of seconds, a sleek black leopard rose up from her haunches. She looked more slender and graceful than the stockier, shorter-tailed jaguars he'd known in his youth. When she shook, a small cloud of black fur mingled with the shifter-mate magic threads that surrounded her like a golden aura.

Only after she rubbed her broad head against his thigh, then disappeared into the thicket, did he realize her clothes had vanished instead of shredding.

In his youth, he'd done it naturally with his first shift. It had taken him months to realize no other shifters in his clan, not even the bull alpha, could shift and return clothes without a magical assist from a spell or charm. At the time, he'd resented it as one more thing that set him apart from the community of seals, but it didn't stop him from taking advantage of it.

The sawing and occasional crashing continued, but instead of growing louder, it moved east. The same direction Chantal had gone.

He didn't need the prodding of his inner beast to contact her via telepathy. *If it's the ekinos, their spines have a paralyzing toxin, and they can shoot them. Don't know how well that works on land.*

Good to know. It's an ekino, but just one. It's like the ones the demesne showed me, but it's missing a leg... arm?

She sent him an image of a battered, slimy-looking ekino using its extended central mouth full of serrated teeth to bite a shrub. It should have had five limbs, but one was a torn stump that oozed yellowish brown ichor, and another looked shredded.

You said they like meat, so my current plan is to use my feline tastiness to lure it into chewing its way around the island perimeter until it bleeds out.

Please be careful. He knew her to be confident rather than cocky, but he worried for her anyway.

To distract himself, he stripped several thin, flexible branches to weave together into a sling. The island had plenty of fist-sized, sharp rocks to use for ammunition. If his sore feet were any indication, he'd probably stepped on half of them.

This thing stinks like five-day-old fish. In the vision from the demesne, the ekino had a control gem above some of its eyes. All this one has is a gaping hole about the size of my paw. She sent him another image to accompany her words. Four of the ten eyes were missing, too.

He tried to remember what Sunscar had told him. *I think that's good and bad. Good because no one can see us through the ekino's eyes or tell it what to do, but bad because there's nothing to stop it from eating everything in its path and regenerating. It can strip a marine valley in less than a month.*

The sawing sound paused, then started again.

Terrific. We need a plan B.

I have an idea. I'm coming to you.

Her path would have been impossible to follow if he didn't already have a sense of where she was. Thankfully, he could walk both fast and quietly as a human. His sloth could be surprisingly stealthy, but not on dry land.

The angle of the afternoon sun meant the trees cast long shadows, which was where he found a crouching black leopard. One furry ear turned his direction.

On the other side of a tangle of shrubs, the ekino's eyes swiveled toward them both. Its chewing stopped for several seconds, then sped up. It was half again as big as Nessireth's had been. The putrid smell threatened to revive his nausea.

He touched her tail. "I'll keep watch while you shift."

It only took a few seconds for Chantal's human form to appear out of a cloud of shifter magic. He'd once been that fast at shifting, and hoped to be again.

She rolled her shoulders back in a graceful stretch. "What do you need me to do?"

Each time he saw her, even if it was after only minutes apart, warmth and longing bloomed in him. Was it ever going to be the right time to tell her?

To cover the upswell of un-warriorlike feelings, he handed her the pink crystal, which she slid into her shirt. "I want to immobilize the ekino long enough to use this." He held up his wrist with the chain.

Her expressive face scrunched in thought for a long moment. "I've got a fishing line with a set of hooks, but they're meant for snagging food fish, not six-foot-tall ekinos." She glanced at the spiny monster, then back to

Dauro. "The line could tie up its extended mouth parts, though. Distract it long enough for the charm to do its thing. Can you work your kinetic magic as a human? You'd have to wrap fast."

He stumbled over the word she used for his pushing magic, until the meaning tumbled into his mind like a forgotten memory.

"I think I can handle the line." In the impossible river, his magic had substituted for fine motor skills his sloth side lacked, but sloths considered speed a waste of perfectly good time. "I don't know about fast."

From the big pocket on her thigh, she pulled out a flat reel and handed it to him. "Hooks are already tied on the outer end." She returned her gaze to the ekino. "I'd offer to zap it with an energy bolt, but it might not work on hellfrog wannabes, and it would wipe out my magic reserves." A disgruntled sound came from her. "Next time I go on a rescue mission, remind me not to skip breakfast."

"I will." It pleased him to think they'd still be together when she needed such a reminder. He handed her the chain from his wrist, then started uncoiling the blue-tinted line with its array of sharp hooks. "Hellfrog?"

"Cross between a frog and an insect, kills and eats whatever the owner points it at, and almost impossible to destroy. A notorious monster-maker named Surasa created them. Based on what he told me, it's an even-odds bet that she made Sunscar, too."

"He told us he was a failed experiment created in a laboratory. He said the rest was none of our business, but I think he was trying to spare us his nightmares." He tested the strength of the uncoiled line with his fingers and the weight with his magic. It felt lighter than a spider web. "I am deeply worried for him."

"Me, too. I hope the flamingos–"

The ekino hissed and began quivering all over. One of the gaping eye sockets bulged with green puffy flesh and flared magic. A white center morphed into a milky white, pupil-less eyeball.

Suddenly, a spine shot out from its body and aimed at Chantal. She dodged, but it grazed her pantleg as it went by.

Instant anger powered his magic. The line flew straight and true and set hooks into the base of the protruding mouth parts. He envisioned wrapping the line like a spider encasing its prey. There was enough extra line to make several loops around the tree trunk the mouth had been chewing on.

Chantal held up the chain. "Ekino," she said, then quickly sang the charm's musical trigger.

Sorcerer magic flared. The slime on the ekino's skin hardened and cracked as the creature struggled. The line stretched but held.

The ekino hissed louder as the oozing yellow blood dried and flaked off. The shredded arm shriveled while the others hardened. Spines shrank and twisted. An unearthly keening sound emitted from the trapped mouth.

"Die, damnit!" said Chantal through gritted teeth.

The chain in her hand was glowing red and smoking. The scent of her charred flesh stung his nose.

Dauro pulled off his tunic to wrap his hand, then picked up the ekino spine. Borrowing strength from his sloth, he hurled the spine like a spear. It impaled the ekino's body in the wound where the control gem had been.

The keening cut off with a sharp, strangled screech.

A strong gust of wind raised a cloud of dust from the creature's frozen form.

Dauro pushed the spine with his magic.

The ekino's body slowly disintegrated into a pyramid of

dust. Another gust blew the dust outward, staining the white sand with brownish gray.

Chantal stood frozen a moment longer, then relaxed. She hissed as she gingerly pried the chain off her badly charred flesh.

He took the still-warm, bloody chain from her. "Can you use your healing spell on yourself?" From personal experience, he knew burns could leave permanent scars.

His tunic looked as clean as when Rosinette had made it, so he unwrapped it from his hand and put it back on. Better to be too hot than a have hundred new scratches from the cursed shrubs. Too bad it wasn't long-sleeved like Chantal's stained but seemingly indestructible shirt.

"Yeah, but I'm going to be *really* sorry I didn't eat." She sighed. "If I faint, don't tell anyone."

He dropped to one knee and patted his leg. "It will be our secret." Hastily, he slipped the chain in his chest pocket, then opened his arms.

She hesitated a moment, then sat on his thigh and snuggled into his loose hold. "You smell way better than ekinos."

He chuckled. "You do, too." Her scent gave him hot thoughts again, but he wasn't passing up the chance to be almost skin to skin with her.

She held the wrist of her injured hand with her other hand. At the top of a deep breath, she closed her eyes. Powerful magic flowed, bathing her hand in concentrated shifter magic and electrifying the threads of shifter-mate magic.

It also sent desire racing through his veins, flushing his chest. Heat coalesced in his groin, raising him instantly to hard and ready.

The sloth side urged him to find out if her taste was as perfect as her scent. His primitive human side wanted to know if her almost pointed ear tip was a pleasure zone. His hips thrust forward involuntarily.

With a temple-pounding effort, he doused all their fantasies with the cold reminder that hunters were still after them. He owed her protection, not lust.

Her magic subsided, leaving only a red stripe across her palm where the flesh had been blackened and oozing. She slumped against him. "Dizzy. Give me a minute."

He tightened his hold. "I've got you."

At the encouragement of his sloth, he whispered a shifter warrior chant from long ago that allowed him to share magical strength with her. Shifter-mate magic threads danced in response, forming brief complex patterns before falling apart.

She shuddered in his arms. "Your magic revs my engines every time." Her arms snaked around his waist. "I'll forget my own name in a minute."

"Same." Nuzzling into her hair, he drew in her scent mixed with sea salt and feminine arousal.

She pulled back to meet his gaze. "I know we're playing with matches near a drought-stricken forest, but I'm dying kiss you."

He cupped the side of her face. "Yes."

Her lips met his halfway.

The taste and scent of her imprinted themselves in every cell of his body. He groaned, or they both did. He wasn't sure. Her tongue engaged him in a slow, sensuous dance for two. His hips twitched forward when her thigh grazed his erect hardness. He had no control around her.

Breaking off the kiss, she gasped for air. "Wow." A smile stole across her face. "You are the best kiss…"

Her expression morphed from blissful to confused as she put her hand to her chest. "The crystal is pulsing." Her other hand cupped the bottom of her breast. "So is the portal pearl."

A gust of wind blew up sand and dust, making him squint. Beyond the trees, over the big island of Vieques, white clouds moved too fast to be natural. "Trouble."

She looked to where he pointed at the expanding funnel of blue and gray. "Dammit." She blew out a noisy breath as she stood up. "Too far for me to sense, but I'll lay odds it's one of the demesne anchors. Maybe the last one."

A stronger gust of wind, almost chilly, blew more sand through the trees. He rose to stand just behind her, not liking the feel of the air. His warrior days were long gone, but the instincts still operated.

Her hand flattened against her shirt, over the crystal. "I suck at telepathy, but I think this thing is trying to talk to me." She turned to face him as she pulled the crystal out to offer it to him. "Or to you."

The moment he touched it, Sunscar's telepathic voice came through loud and fast. *Chantal! Dauro! The fairies opened a new portal. The demesne is dying.*

Slow down, thought Dauro. He caught Chantal's other hand with his to strengthen the connection between them.

Why did the fairies need a new portal? asked Chantal.

I penned up the hunters in the castle with the fairies. I was going to give you another day, then *quit terrorizing them so they could leave.*

He sent a montage of terrified hunters running from him, fearful and angry hunters standing at the castle entrance, and the walkway and lawn full of their big, empty trucks.

The river started sloshing like a bathtub, and the castle sent a statue to ask me for help. The fairies linked with the hunters' wizard to punch a hole through the castle to create a new portal. The castle says the demesne's magic is bleeding out.

Can you leave by the same portal? asked Dauro.

Might not be safe, said Chantal. *The storm over Vieques could tear him apart.* She sent an image of the ominous, tornadic clouds laced with lightning.

I wouldn't go anyway. Sunscar's thoughts sounded almost sheepish. *I promised the castle I'd help.*

Okay, thought Chantal, *here's my off-the-wall idea. Sunscar asks the castle and the demesne if they can redirect the new portal to our little island. I use the pearl and my magic to stabilize it. Dauro contacts Nibi to tell her what we're doing, then we go in and ask the demesne and the castle to tell us how to help them.*

Sunscar was silent a moment. *The castle agrees. Activate the portal pearl so the demesne can find you. I'm going inside the castle. I'll contact you when we're ready on our end.* His presence in their minds vanished.

Chantal squeezed Dauro's fingers. "Are you okay with this?"

"No. I want you safe, but we need your talents to save Sunscar, and we can't wait for a better path." He stepped closer, so the only thing separating them was the flat crystal. "Are you okay with this?"

"Yes. I wish I could send you somewhere safe, too, but I don't know where that would be, and, as you said, we need to rescue Sunscar. Helping people is what I do." She surprised him with a quick, hard kiss. "Find someone to tell about our plans."

Though she hid it well, he sensed her worry and doubt. She started to pull away.

"Wait." He kept his expression serious. "If anyone asks, what plan letter are we on?"

She snorted with laughter. "Plan C, for crazy."

Chantal warily watched the arched portal as it wove an uneven pattern around the island shrubs. On the far side, she could only see a dark hallway lit by the fading sunlight from the real world. Her head pounded with the effort to keep the portal stable, even with the help of the uncomfortably hot portal pearl tucked in her bra. Bless Rosinette's musical magic for making its activation spell unforgettable.

Thankfully, Dauro was already returning from his quick swim to make contact with Nibi. She'd felt his approach before she heard him forcing his way through the hell-spawn bushes. Despite her best intentions for taking their relationship slowly and deliberately, their connection grew stronger with each passing hour. If he decided he didn't want her in his life, it would hurt like hell.

Moments later, he appeared, just as twilight started to take hold. "The flamingos found Nibi, Rosinette, and the others. They also have the specialist standing by where the hunters entered the portal this morning." He handed her the charmed chain. Based on his bone-dry clothes and hair, he'd obviously used it to good effect after leaving the water.

"I'm glad they're safe. We need all the support we can get." She slipped the chain into the bag with the other treasures she carried for the group. "Ready?"

Dauro took the hand she offered, then stepped closer to face her. "It may be the wrong time to speak of it, but I'm not missing the chance again. I love you."

She tried to tell herself that he meant it like he loved his friends, but she knew it was more. Felt it in her beat-skipping heart. "I want to–"

Fairy magic spasmed and lanced pain through her head. The portal glowed blindingly bright. The pearl in her bra stung her breast like a white-hot ember, and the crystal in her shirt heated.

She fought to keep control. "We have to go now."

He nodded once, then turned and released her hand to link his elbow with hers. They walked through quickly together.

The crystal felt like a furnace against her stomach as they cleared the portal that closed behind them with a pressure-popping snap. Chill settled in her bones in the inky blackness.

Dauro blew out a loud breath. "I can't contact Sunscar through your shield."

"What if lowering it makes you go slothy on me? That would be three forced shifts in one day for you." Their voices echoed in the silent hall.

"The demesne promised Sunscar not to enforce the rule." His confident tone was belied by the undercurrent of unease she felt via their connection.

"Okay, but don't squish me with your magnificent furry self." She let the shield go and breathed a sigh of relief when he stayed human.

He probably felt her worry through their connection, but he was sweet enough to pretend he didn't notice. The same way she pretended not to notice his undeniable fear of returning to his prison.

Light suddenly blazed brightly about fifty feet in front of them, illuminating a rectangular shape on the wall.

"That's for us," said Dauro. He caught her hand in his as they walked briskly down the hall. Her headache faded with each step, but her stomach reminded her she hadn't eaten all day.

The light turned out to be another portal, this one barely wide enough for one person to slip through sideways. On the other side stood Sunscar, impatiently waving them forward. "Quickly. We're out of time."

She shushed her possessive inner leopard and let go of Dauro's hand. "I'm right behind you."

He side-stepped through and headed for Sunscar.

The moment she stepped through, the portal vanished with a tiny flare of light and magic.

Once again, they were in the castle's big hall of broken cabinets, torn tapestries, and charms scattered everywhere. One charred wall now had a web of spider cracks in the stone. Unsurprisingly, no one had cleaned up the mess.

Before Sunscar could say another word, Dauro enveloped him in a long bear hug. "Thank you for helping us all escape."

Sunscar pushed himself back and scowled. "Wraiths don't hug."

"Of course not," said Chantal. Sunscar's arms had been just as tight around Dauro. "You're very terrifying."

A tremor passed through the castle floor. Empty plastic water bottles rolled and danced.

The castle's disembodied voice echoed through the hall. "Go to the bridge."

Sunscar turned and glided toward the exit, his feet not quite touching the ground. She and Dauro followed with alacrity. Being crushed by a collapsing fairy castle wouldn't be a pleasant way to die.

Outside, they had to dodge the hunters' big trucks left haphazardly in the front yard. Gusts of wind tried to steal their breath as they ran toward the bridge. The sun looked like a pink watercolor smear in the sky.

At the top of the bridge, the statue of the small, malevolent cherub beckoned stiffly.

Sunscar scowled. "Fairy magic is clusterfucked."

Chantal laughed at his disgruntled tone. "Magic is magic. Fairies are fairies."

The cherub's jaw dropped like a nutcracker's, revealing serpent-like fangs. "Open the guest portal here," said the castle's voice.

The ground shook, making it a challenge to stay on her feet. Below the bridge, the river looked choppy and swollen.

As she slowed, she opened her senses to the demesne magic. Alien anguish and fear poured into her. She'd have fallen to her knees if Dauro hadn't been there to catch her and pull her close.

Struggling to shape her thoughts as magic, she tried to send comfort with words. *We're bringing someone in to help you.*

"Open portal here," demanded the cherub.

The ground shook. The wide, heavy stone bridge swayed.

She spoke the activation spell as fast as she could. Pain lanced through her head, making her dizzy. She leaned into Dauro's solid strength. "Pearl, please open the external guest portal to this location."

"Portal commencing."

Magic coalesced. Winds increased to gale force as a ring formed.

Dauro grabbed Sunscar's arm to save him from blowing over the side of the bridge's railing. He pulled both her and Sunscar back to the foot of the bridge.

The surging magic made her bones ache. Demesne magic sparked, then spun out of control like a bag of lit firecrackers. She fought to form an image of a wide door, urgently asking the demesne to solidify the outline.

The demesne tried to help, but there weren't enough threads. She poured as much of her free magic as she could muster into the image, but only the frame solidified. The door itself remained stubbornly insubstantial.

A cold lump formed in her stomach. Her magic wasn't enough. She'd failed. She'd doomed Dauro and Sunscar to die with the mortally wounded demesne that had held them captive for so long. She sank to her knees.

The next thing she knew, she was wrapped in Dauro's warm embrace. *Use my strength. Use my magic.*

The demesne's anguish and her own despair crushed her hope. *I don't know how.*

Your leopard does. We're mates, blessed by the Heart of the Sky. Dauro sent her a wave of love so strong it brought tears to her eyes. *I want to live with you. Love you. Bond with me, and together, we'll open the clusterfucking portal.*

Want and need swelled in her, overwhelming her rational brain's stubborn insistence that shifters couldn't bond without the physical connection of making love. Golden shifter-mate magic threads didn't lie. *This is for life. Are you sure?*

Yes. His hold tightened around her. *By the moon and the ocean, yes. By the sun and the wind, yes.*

Tears streamed down her face, but she didn't care. "I love you. Yes."

Her shifter magic twined with his, gold threads weaving a sinuous glowing cord between and around them.

Magic and strength flowed through her, washing away fears and doubts. Chantal and her leopard fused with Dauro and his sloth, becoming one for a long moment, then returning, each with a piece of the other in their shared hearts.

The ground shook. Overhead, the pink sun leaked watercolor rivulets as the sky dimmed.

The cherub emitted a high-pitched whistle. "Warning! Warning! Portal failure!"

Clinging to Dauro and meshing her magic with his, she helped the demesne stabilize the door and connect to the real world.

Sunscar grounded his feet and fought the winds to climb the bridge to the portal. A translucent field blocked his hand from reaching through into the darkness.

"Key required!" shouted the cherub.

"The crystal," said Dauro. "Nessireth didn't trust anyone."

He helped her to her feet. Together, with their arms wrapped around each other, they forced their way up the bridge.

She pulled the crystal out of her shirt and put it in Sunscar's hands. "You need this."

As he stepped toward the portal, she asked the demesne to open the door. The translucent field faded. Dark winds howled from the sudden opening, blowing a cloud of dust right into her face.

Fairy magic flared from the other side. A slender hand reached through. "A little help here!"

Sunscar stepped into the threshold, holding the glowing pink crystal. With his free hand, he grabbed the outstretched hand and pulled.

A slender figure slammed into Sunscar, sending him staggering back into Dauro's solid bulk.

"Close portal!" demanded the cherub.

Chantal struggled to visualize shrinking the portal opening like a camera shutter. The portal pearl in her bra burned like fire. Despite Dauro's added strength, the portal fought to widen.

A powerful wave of fairy magic smoothed over the doorway and erased it completely. The wind stopped abruptly.

"There, that's better," said the fairy as she disentangled her long, varicolored curly hair from Sunscar's silvery coils. "Thanks for the assist."

Fine red dust coated everything. Chantal sneezed so hard she stumbled into Dauro. He caught and held her while she tried to find where she stashed her bandana. Her eyes watered and stung from the dusty grit.

"Who are you?" Sunscar's tone mixed challenge and respect.

"Zephyr." The voice sounded irrepressibly cheerful. "You can be none other than the gorgeous but grumbly Sunscar."

Chantal looked up in surprise, blinking to clear the haze. "Any relation to wind fairy Magister Zephyr of the legendary Battle of Siroc Academy?"

"Ah, the price of fame," said Zephyr. "Stop one djinn army from taking over a school, and they graduate you to get rid of you. As if I brought the invasion. I'm only part wind fairy, by the way. I am enchanted to meet the noble Dauro and intrepid Chantal. Nice work with the portal."

"Can you fix the demesne?" asked Sunscar.

"Maybe," said Zephyr. She pointed to the cherub. "Tell me about the rock magic."

"I think the castle and the demesne are symbiotic."

Sunscar held up the crystal. "The castle has the logic, and the demesne has the… heart, if that's the right word."

Zephyr's eyes widened in surprise. "Fascinating. Probably explains why it didn't implode. This will be fantastic. I can't wait!"

Chantal couldn't help but smile at Zephyr's enthusiasm. "Can you let Dauro and Sunscar out? They don't deserve to be imprisoned a moment longer."

"Collectors," said Zephyr with deep disgust. "Makes you ashamed to have fairy heritage, doesn't it?"

Dauro grumbled low in his chest.

Zephyr held up her hands apologetically. "No offense meant to your new mate. All the ancient races have collectors. Or worse." She cast her gaze upward at the remaining streaks of the fading pink sun. "Give a minute." Waves of fairy magic began flowing from her.

Sunscar turned to stare at Dauro, jaw dropped. "You're mated? Why didn't I know? Why didn't you tell me?" He glared at them both. "And why can't I read your thoughts anymore?"

Dauro smiled. "I don't love you any less because I've fallen in love with a kind and clever leopard woman. I no longer take my gifts for granted." He snugged his arms around Chantal. "The Heart of the Sky has shared with me her gift for shielding, including mind speech."

She turned in his arms to look up at him. "Really?" She hoped he'd teach her how to use her shield for herself.

He kissed her. "Yes."

She'd have felt his love even if he hadn't pulsed their mate bond open when their lips touched. Which immediately revved her hormones into overdrive.

Cupping his beloved face with her hands, she returned the kiss with interest. The taste of him rocked through her core. *My leopard demands that I drag you off to our lair and play with your naked body. Does the castle have a bed?*

He chuckled and nuzzled her ear, making her nipples diamond hard and aching for his touch. *My sloth wants to sing to announce our territory, then slow-walk you to a thousand orgas—*

"Okay," said Zephyr. "Here's the situation."

Chantal dragged her attention back to the fairy and tried not to resent the interruption.

"This place has enough stored magic to rip open reality and make it bleed. The demesne needs a new conductor, which can be me for a while, but I can't handle the living rock." A grimace flitted across her expressive face. "The castle knows and trusts its charges, meaning any of you six who were in the collection. I imagine none of you want that job until we can get a trustworthy rock specialist, but without one, I can only slow the inevitable demise."

Sunscar's shoulders squared. "I will stay."

Dauro's alarm and dismay echoed across their mate bond. "I don't care what that dung-throwing witch said, you are not a sacrificial goat! Your life is your own."

Sunscar waved placatingly toward Dauro. "I won't stay forever. Just until the specialist gets here." He closed his eyes for a long moment. "I've seen the real world. It's not yet ready for me."

Chantal suspected it was the other way around, but Sunscar was finally free to make his own choices. She wouldn't try to tell him what to do. "If you want to just visit, Kotoyeesinay would be a safe place to go. I'll introduce you to the laughing wraith."

"Speaking of your hometown," said Zephyr. "The demesne has one failing anchor left. We can add more here, or we can move the demesne to someplace that's not in the path of Category Five hurricanes. I was thinking one of the sanctuary towns would be the best shot at finding new permanent owners. Kotoyeesinay would be great."

Chantal shook her head. "Way above my pay grade. I'm just a deputy sheriff. I'll introduce you to the town council." She tilted her chin toward Sunscar. "If there's any justice, the demesne should benefit the former captives."

"Good idea." Zephyr beamed, then frowned. "I wish I could port you there directly, but it's going to take decades to find all the portal blocks Nessireth hid around the island. She was one paranoid fairy." Zephyr pointed at Chantal's chest. "If you give me the pearl node, I'll open the guest entrance on top of the hill. The flamingos should be still waiting, if they haven't gotten distracted."

"Gladly." Chantal dug in her bra for the still-warm portal pearl and handed it to the fairy. "I'm probably going to have burn scars for days."

Zephyr squinted as she examined it. "That shouldn't have… oh, I see. Its secondary shell is Alfar metal. What an odd choice."

"Probably meant to deter one of us from stealing it." Dauro shook his head. "Nessireth had thousands of years to dream up things like that. Ask Rosinette to lend you the book."

"And you're dreaming if you think a wyvern is giving up a book of magic." Zephyr laughed. "I'm negotiating for copies of selected pages."

"Not to be rude or anything," said Chantal, "but is now a good time to open the portal? I haven't eaten all day. I can't even smell my mate because of Nessireth's stupid scent-suppression rules built into the demesne. Dauro deserves to be free and stay that way."

"Oh, right." Zephyr held up the pearl with one hand and waved Sunscar toward the bridge with the other. "Do me a favor and go tell the cloud-fairy statue it's okay."

Chantal was glad she'd never compared an actual cloud fairy to a malevolent cherub. It likely wouldn't have gone well for her.

Sunscar glided to the top of the bridge to put a hand on the statue's head. After a moment, he nodded.

Zephyr blinked once slowly. A tiny whorl of magic grew to a spinning circle, then settled on the walkway. The center faded to black. Beyond the portal, light from the demesne spilled like a giant search beam onto the dirt and rocks of Vieques.

A faint voice came from the other side. "Magister? Are you okay?"

"We're just ducky, thanks. Sending two through. The eye-candy wraith is staying to help for a bit." Zephyr nodded to Chantal and Dauro and pointed her thumb toward the portal. "Thank you for flying Zephyr Air."

"Wait," said Dauro. "How can we talk to you and Sunscar once you close the portal?"

"Oh, good point." Zephyr's eyebrows furrowed in thought. "I can hop sound and image through a plane or two to get to Earth, but Sunscar should have his own means."

Chantal considered her resources. "I'm carrying a 'find-me' paired set of a bracelet and charm. Feels like witch magic. Could we build on it to make a trans-plane connector?" She opened the bag of treasures and pulled them out for Zephyr to see.

Zephyr nodded. "I can work with that, if you can handle the charm part of the magic."

"I'm not as good as my mother, but I think I can tease apart the magic so you can lay in the end points."

Zephyr looked to Sunscar. "Tell the rock... castle what we're about."

Sunscar's chest thrust out in affront. "I already did."

Zephyr turned her face away, but not before Chantal saw her rolling her eyes.

The paired charm proved well made, so it only took Chantal a few seconds to open the ethereal magical connection. Meanwhile, Zephyr spun demesne threads into an elegant, complex line. Together, they coiled it into the charm's magic, and Chantal sealed it shut.

Chantal slipped her hand into Dauro's. "Come set the ringtone."

Together they climbed the bridge to where Sunscar hovered near the cherubic cloud-fairy statue.

Chantal held out her hand. "Both of you touch the charm and the bracelet. Say a phrase in unison. You each take one. Whenever one of you says that phrase, it'll open a nano-portal with your voice and image to the other." She blew out a breath. "That's the theory, anyway. If it doesn't work, Zephyr promises to work with my mother to make one that does."

"You pick the phrase," said Dauro.

Sunscar looked away for a moment, then back again with a slight smile. "I finally get to teach you Shakespeare. 'We are such stuff as dreams are made on.'"

Hands clasped, with the charm in between, they repeated Sunscar's phrase.

As she'd hoped, the witch and demesne magic sparked, then settled.

Sunscar took the charm as something he could put on a necklace. Dauro settled the bracelet on his wrist. Chantal helped it conform to his size with a tiny flare of magic.

"Go now," said Sunscar. With a suspicious glance toward Zephyr, he lowered his voice. "Fairies aren't known for their patience."

Zephyr laughed. "True. But we are known for our fantastic hearing."

Dauro wrapped Sunscar in a tight hug. "I owe you my life, and I love you. Call me anytime, anywhere."

Sunscar nodded. "I will call." He turned to Chantal. "Congratulations on your mating. You are blessed to have found each other."

"Yes, I am. You're a good friend." She stifled her impulse to hug him herself to thank him for all he'd done. Physical contact seemed to startle him.

Zephyr cleared her throat loudly. "Not to be an *impatient fairy* or anything, but the flamingos are afraid I've lost you in another dimension."

Chantal held out her hand. "Come, my beloved, sexy mate, let's go brave the new world."

He took her hand with a smile. "Yes."

Zephyr waved cheerfully as they stepped through her portal into the chilly, windy night of Vieques. The portal snapped shut.

Flashlights and lanterns revealed not only a number of flamingo shifters, but all the rest of Dauro's fellow captives. They swarmed him with hugs, laughter, and questions.

Chantal stood aside. She couldn't help but smile like a loon at the happiness radiating from them all and through her mate bond with Dauro.

Leticia stepped closer. "How are you doing?" She waggled a finger. "And don't just say 'okay,' or I'll have the whole town of Kotoyeesinay here on the next portal and fast boat."

Chantal snorted in amusement. "Hungry. Exhausted. Filthy. Floating on air. People were rescued." Real-world smells reminded her of real-world problems. "Did you find the fairies and the hunters?"

"Yes, their escape hatch dumped them in the ocean about twenty kilometers offshore." Leticia pointed toward the chattering former captives. "The capricorns told us where to look. We got help from the Shifter Tribunal office in Florida to pull *los idiotas* out of the water. Rock fairies don't float."

"Did the wild magic storm cause any more damage?"

"No, we lucked out there. It looked like a killer, but it wasn't quite in the real world yet. It faded fast, right about the time you and Dauro went back into the demesne." Leticia chuckled. "The few humans who noticed it were drunk on Puerto Rican rum. That's our story, and we're sticking to it."

Chantal's inner leopard reminded her of unfinished business with her mate. Hell, not-even-started business. "Could I ask a huge favor and not answer any questions about it?"

Leticia's expression turned serious. "It depends. Ask me."

Chantal stuck her hands in her pockets. "A quiet place for me and Dauro with lots of food, a shower, a bed, and privacy for a couple of days?"

The older woman didn't even hesitate. "Give me an hour, and I'll drive you there myself." She pulled out her satellite radio and stepped away.

All the shifters had already seen the mate bond, so Chantal wasn't giving away anything by saying Dauro's name. But she and Dauro desperately needed to work things out between them before they faced the rest of the world.

The Jeep slowed to a stop. "This is it."

Dauro felt like he was dream-flying. Exhilaration mixed with wonder and the deep-seated fear that he'd wake up any moment and find himself back in Nessireth's demesne, drifting in the impossible river.

Chantal ignored the passenger door and swung up and over the side to land on the dirt driveway.

He mimicked her rather than figure out how the door handle worked.

"Amazing." Chantal turned to Leticia, who was still behind the wheel of the noisy vehicle. "I'm afraid to ask how many favors you had to call in for this."

Beyond the Jeep's headlights, a series of low lights led to a two-story wood and glass cabin nestled in the jungle. Strings of tiny lights outlined nearly ever post and beam, inside and out. No fairy magic anywhere, so the lights had to be technology.

"Not too many." Leticia pulled a backpack from the footwell and handed it to Chantal. "Supplies. Someone will come get you Thursday morning. Radio if you need anything."

With that, she backed out of the short driveway and drove off.

Chantal shouldered the backpack's strap and held out her other hand to him. "Let's go in. I smell food."

He gladly wrapped his hand around hers and walked the path with her.

The cozy cabin had clear glass walls everywhere except for the smoke-colored walls of the bathroom. The small, open kitchen's counters were nearly invisible under the many trays covered in thin, clear film… plastic wrap.

Chantal dropped the backpack on the floor, then closed the cabin's door. "I want to set some magic wards. Then we need to talk, and we need to eat. And I need a shower because I stink like salt-cured roadkill. Which do you want to do first?"

"Let's eat and talk at the same time." The nervousness she'd been trying to hide made him uneasy.

Breathing deeply and slowly, her eyes closed. Her lips moved in soundless words. Magic flared and settled in the windows and door like a glaze of frost.

"Okay." Her eyes opened. "We'll hear warning tones if anything bigger than a lizard tries to get in."

"Good." He kicked himself. He should have been thinking of security, not his worries.

Delectable smells filled the room as she uncovered the trays. "What do you like?"

"I don't know." The variety on the trays seemed endless, and none of it familiar. "Anything that isn't nutrient-enhanced sea grass."

Laughing, she handed him a plate with a knife and a tiny metal trident. "You go first."

After crowding his plate with as many samples as he

could, they sat in ornate metal chairs at the small round metal table. The first few bites nearly overwhelmed him with flavor, but his human senses soon settled down and let him savor the new tastes. Maybe he'd have favorites someday, but for now, they all tasted intriguingly different.

Chantal's choices leaned toward meat, eggs, and fruit. After bolting down a small steak in record time, she opened cabinets in the kitchen until she found two glasses, then brought them each water.

"So, talking." She used her trident... fork to hold a piece of chicken while she cut pieces with her knife. "I don't know where to start, so I'm just going to muddle through. First, I am your mate, and you are mine, and I love you. I want you so much I'm shaking. I want to make love with you so you smell like me and I smell like you." She sighed. "But you've just spent centuries as a captive, and I'm afraid our bond will be trading one prison for another. Because we were blessed with telepathy first, I know intellectually it was our choice together, but my heart says I took advantage of you."

Relief that she wasn't pushing him away flooded him. Rolling his shoulders back slowly helped ease his tension and let air into his lungs. "I want to help my friends find their families, and see the new world. There's so much to learn." He paused, waiting for her to look at him again. "I don't want to be your cage, either. I love you too much for that."

She opened her mouth to speak, then seemed to think better of it. Finally, she shook her head. "Our relationship is unbalanced right now. Only time can change that."

The gods had blessed him with a mate with wisdom beyond her tender years. And for all his ancient years, he only had the wisdom of civilization long gone and the instincts of his somnolent sloth.

Quiet settled as he finished his samples. Chantal ate like she thought the food would get away. He appreciated the time to think about their problem.

He aligned his fork next to the square edge of his empty plate. "I liked what you said about shifter-mate magic being potential, not destiny. In my time, true-mate pairings were considered divine gifts from the gods. If a union failed, it was because the gods withdrew their favor." He reached across the table to cover her hand with his own. "But if it's both blessing and biology, then it's up to us to make our bond work. To listen instead of relying on instinct. To ask with words instead of silence."

In answer, she leaned forward to lift and brush his knuckles with a quick kiss. "Sounds good to me. My dad's trucking business takes him away a lot, so he and my mom make a point of talking about things together instead of bottling up the grievances until they explode."

He squeezed her fingers. "I'd like to meet them, when you're ready."

She grinned, acknowledging his teasing repetition of her earlier words. "Any time."

He stood and picked up his empty plate. "I take it our union won't start a clan war, then?"

"Nope. Everyone will be delighted. They think I'm too solitary." After a last swallow of water, she collected everything else on the table and led him to the kitchen.

"Let's put the dishes in the sink for now." She pointed her knee toward a rectangular metal door under the counter. "I'll show you the wonderful invention called a dishwasher later." Her nose wrinkled. "Right now, I want out of these stinky clothes." Her lips curved into an overly innocent smile. "Would you like to help me with that?"

Simmering desire rose. "It would be my pleasure." He caressed her shoulder, sliding his hand to her neck. She leaned in and up for a long, sensuous kiss. As much as he'd enjoyed the flavors of the new world, he would never get enough of the taste of her.

Under his lips, she laughed. "You think the nicest things." Her hand slid into his as she stepped back. "Let's take the backpack upstairs and see what the flamingos gave us."

A bedroom took up the entire second floor, which Chantal called a loft. The largest bed he'd ever seen butted up against a frosted-glass wall. The other walls had regular windows.

She unhooked the radio holster and three other pouches from her belt with sure movements and put them on a decorative table. With less ceremony, she dumped the backpack's contents onto the bed, then sat next to the pile and sorted through it deftly. She held up one of several shiny square packets. "Bless them for their thoughtfulness."

No stray memories appeared. "What are they?"

"Condoms. Birth control. Very thin sheath for a man's penis." Her shoulder lifted. "We don't need them, though. I have a charm that prevents pregnancy. More reliable than human methods for two shifters."

He couldn't imagine how they worked. "How do they stay on?"

She tossed the packet on the bed. "They stretch." She raised a foot and untied the bow of her boot lace and grinned up at him. "Wanna get hot and wet with me in the shower?"

In answer, he stripped his tunic, pants, and shoes off in seconds. "I could help you get out of all those clothes."

Laughing as she kicked off her boot, she shook her head. "I'd never finish. You're too tempting. Were you always built like a sexy god who owns his own fitness center?"

He raised an arm and glanced at the muscle. "Not this much, that I remember. Maybe it came from my sloth. I cajoled him into swimming the entire river each day instead of just grazing the sea grass and sleeping in my nest. Nessireth thought I was patrolling."

Chantal made a rude sound. "She was an idiot. You were making friends. Finding people to love." Her other boot joined the first, followed by her socks. She wriggled her toes as she speedily unbuttoned her long-sleeved shirt.

"Are you jealous?" Even as he spoke his concern, he watched hungrily as she shed her shirt. The light tan of her undertunic... camisole set off the beauty of her rich brown skin.

Her movements slowed. "I'd say I'm possessive about what's mine, but not of people. Your open heart is the heart of you." She dropped the filthy shirt on top of her boots and quickly unzipped and stepped out of her even filthier pants. "How could I not love you?" The sincerity shining in her bright eyes and soft smile allayed his worry.

A moment later, her nude form bared, all he could do was bask in her beauty. Graceful shoulders and well-defined arm muscles. Pillowy breasts with dark, jutting nipples. Narrow waist, wide and perfectly rounded stomach and hips, muscular thighs, and a thick thatch of dark pubic hair that made his mouth water.

A smile stole across her face as she picked up a bar of soap and a small bottle. "Let's see if the shower is big enough for two."

He followed her like a fish in school into the shiny room with frosted-glass walls. Tiny mirrors everywhere reflected their passage in fragments. Memories tumbled in his head, trying to tell him about tile and modern plumbing, but all his attention centered on Chantal.

She set the bottle on a small shelf, then turned knobs. Suddenly water rained down on her from a spout. Turning to face it, she slid her cupped hands up to push water under her breasts. He'd never seen a more erotic sight.

At her beckoning gesture, he stepped over the curb and into the spray with her. She turned and wrapped herself around him.

Skin to skin with his mate, his telepathic barriers melted away like sand.

Now, he could feel that she wanted him as much as he wanted her. Muscles in her belly rippled, stroking his erection captured between them. Her soft lips and gentle teeth nibbled their way toward his nipple.

Oceans roared in his ears. Shifter mate magic threads overwhelmed his vision. Tingling began at the base of his spine. "Too fast," he gasped.

She stilled in his arms. "What do you need, my mate?"

"I don't know." Hissing out a ragged breath, he clutched her tight and stepped back with her, out of the spray. "I haven't been human for four hundred years. It's too much. Two thrusts and I'll erupt. And no thrusts at all if you use any of your magic. It fires my blood."

One of her hands inched higher. "We could try sloth slow, one touch at a time." Her breath tickled his shoulder. "Or we can blow your volcano right now. I'm sure we could find something to keep us occupied while you to replenish your lava."

He couldn't help but smile. "My lava?"

She looked up at him with a sly smile. "Seemed fitting."

He lowered his head to barely brush her lips with his. "What if I make you erupt first?" He sent her an image of what he had in mind.

Her small gasp told him the idea pleased her. "I'd love your tongue anywhere I can get it, but I'm filthy."

"Let me take care of that." He gently turned her around in his arms so she faced the warm water.

Using his chin, he pushed her damp hair aside and nuzzled her neck. She didn't need magic. Her scent alone was enough to make his groin twitch.

He took the soap from her hand and rubbed it in small circles over her back. She smelled like mint and midnight frost. The soap smelled like oil and fruit. The tension in her shoulders relaxed.

Gliding his hand around to the side, he slid the soap up under her arm, then circled her breast. He grazed her nipple several times before reaching across to give her other nipple the same treatment.

"Oh, yes," she breathed. Her delight became his through their telepathic link.

Concentrating on pleasing her kept his own body under control. He let his hand drift into the water, then down to the thatch over her mound and lower still into the secrets hidden there. She shuddered with pleasure.

He stepped them both around under the shower head to rinse the soap from her skin, then turned her to face him. "You are a goddess."

The corners of her lips lifted in a languid smile. "You bet your ass."

He gently leaned her back against the glass wall, then sank to crouch in front of her, licking at her wet nipple on his way down. The scent of her arousal led him to nose through her damp curls and inhale.

She moaned and widened her stance when his fingers brushed her soft gate and his tongue found her pearl. He ignored the memories that tried to tell him the anatomical names. This was the poetry of his mate's pleasure, not modern science.

The taste of her, the clutch of her fingers on his shoulders, the connection between them made him fight for control.

Pointing his tongue, he flicked it around and across the enlarged pearl. He slid one finger inside her channel, then two, gently stretching the tight passage.

She moaned again. Her hips twitched toward his face in rhythm with his tongue and fingers. His aching staff twitched right along with her.

Shifter-mate magic threads beckoned seductively, but he closed his senses to them. He wasn't going there without his mate.

Chantal's world had shrunk to Dauro's scent, Dauro's mouth, and the exquisite tension between her legs. Her nipples ached. Her stomach quivered. A storm of visible shifter magic swirled around them and danced on Dauro's skin and hers. But it didn't feel right.

She slid her palm to his face. "Join with me, Dauro. Come inside me."

His serious brown eyes met hers. "I won't last."

"Neither will I. But this first time, I can't take my pleasure before my mate's." She tilted her head back. "Here against the wall, middle of the bed, hanging from the ceiling, wherever, but we should be one."

He got to one knee, then rose slowly, keeping sensuous skin-to-skin contact with her until he stood. His erection pulsed against her belly.

In one swift movement, he lifted her like she weighed nothing and positioned himself at her entrance. She leaned back against the glass and tilted her hips.

One perfect thrust and he was in her, stretching her, filling her, completing her.

Her moan synchronized with his. Shifter-mate magic tightened around them, energizing the bond.

She dropped one hand between them to rapidly stroke her wet and swollen clit. "Come with me, my love."

His eyes flashed sea green as he held her waist and slid out and in with like a piston.

Sparks of magic engulfed them in flames. She spasmed once, twice, and she was gone, lost in a sea of sensation. He shouted with his last, deep thrust and bathed her channel with waves of wet heat.

Her leopard danced, his sloth twirled, and mate magic added unbreakable strands to the complex woven threads they already shared.

Even in her bliss, she could tell their scents were changing, taking on parts of each other, blending new ones that would tell the magical world of their true bond.

Aftershocks of pleasure coursed through her and echoed in him.

She opened her eyes to find herself grinning as she looked into the fathomless brown eyes of the shifter she loved. "Hi."

He returned her smile. "Hello, my mate."

She wanted to stay there forever, with her legs folded tightly around his hips, holding him inside her, but the real world annoyingly didn't care. "We're running out of hot water." Tilting her head toward the still-running shower. "I'd really like to have clean hair when I make love with you again."

He kissed her forehead, then tilted his hips away from hers and slowly set her down on the floor.

Embarrassingly, she had to lock her knees to keep them from wobbling when he stepped back.

Worry settled on his face. "Did I hurt you?"

A chuckle escaped her. "No, just the opposite. I've never had an orgasm like that in my life." She glanced at his semitumescent erection. "I'm pretty sure I'm going to want another one soon for comparison."

He smiled and shook his head. "How do you always know how to make me laugh?"

Her knees didn't betray her this time as she bent to pick up the soap to put it on a small shelf. "Goddess powers."

"Ah, that must be it." The twitching of his lips belied his suitably worshipful mien.

She scooped the shampoo bottle from the shelf and poured a dollop into her hand. "You're a god, too, you know. Your power is love. And making people feel safe."

His expression turned thoughtful as he stepped back and leaned against the glass wall.

She used the hand-held showerhead to wash between her legs, hurriedly scrubbed the shampoo into her scalp and massaged it through her hair. Once would have to do unless she wanted to rinse in chilly water. The rapidly cooling spray washed the sullen suds away.

When she shut off the water and turned around, Dauro stepped in to wrap her with a towel from the nearby rack.

"In my time, the Heart of the Sky was the most powerful of all the gods." He kissed her tenderly. "The Heart has blessed me in more ways than I'll ever know."

She raised her hands to cup his beloved face. "This is your time, now." She rose up on her toes to kiss his generous mouth. "This is our blessed day. Night. Whatever." She kissed him again with slow and sensuous promise.

He matched her intent with a firm caress of her butt and the slow grind of his hips against hers. "Can we try the bed this time? I think I'll need to work up to hanging from the ceiling."

She chuckled. "The bed, yes. Lie down and let me worship at your altar." Sending him her intent was as easy as breathing through their shining mate bond.

The next thing she knew, she was being carried with shifter speed to the king-sized bed.

She grinned as he set her carefully down and vaulted over her to lie on his back beside her. He splayed his legs and folded his hands under his neck, just as she'd imagined in the image she'd shared.

From the collection of toiletries at the edge of the bed, she fished out the bottle of massage oil. The clever flamingos thought of everything.

Out of nowhere, a yawn ambushed her. She refused to give in. Mate time was too precious to waste on sleep.

Dauro sat up and caught her hand. "We have two days full of hours." He took the bottle from her hand. "What I'd really like... okay, my sloth and I would like, is to sleep with you. Making love is great, but naps"—he grabbed two pillows and handed one to her—"are sublime."

A laugh escaped her. "My inner leopard agrees one thousand percent."

She took back the bottle of oil and shoved it and everything else into the backpack. Without thinking, she used a tiny bit of magic to flip the light switch. Motive magic had never come so easily before. Maybe she'd picked it up from the bond. In which case, she'd totally won the mate lottery with Dauro.

When she turned back to the bed, she discovered Dauro had been busy. "You made us a pillow fort."

"It's the closest I could come to a nest." He patted the spot next to him. "Our mate bed will need more pillows."

Her inner leopard quashed her busy little human brain that wanted to talk and plan. "It's perfect, as long as you're in it."

She crawled into the nest as he slid back and held up the sheet for them.

Curling into his living, breathing warmth felt like

coming home. His scent soothed her like no other. Another yawn crept up on her.

"Let us share breath and dreams." His voice rumbled in his chest and vibrated her ear.

"Yes," she murmured, letting sleep take her. "Together."

CHAPTER 14

The last place Dauro ever hoped to be again was old Nessireth's demesne, and yet there he was. He suspected Nibi and Rosinette felt the same way, and yet there they were, too.

His two friends sat together on one of the bridge pathway's stone benches, with a long, plain wooden box on the seat between them. Rosinette's nose was buried in her new e-reader that somehow held a thousand books.

Nibi grinned at him as she patted the bench. "Sit with us. Pacing won't make your mate get here any faster."

Sunscar, hovering near the castle's forest-giant statue, grounded himself and crossed his arms. He looked more plausibly human than he ever had, except he refused to wear clothes and his long silver-gray coils of hair still moved like a tangle of miniature eels. That, and the statues followed him around like ducklings.

Zephyr jumped down from the top of the bridge's side column, landing as if she'd only been three feet up instead of fifteen.

A wave of fairy magic tickled his senses. A circle grew into a glowing arc several yards in front of him.

Zephyr strode to the portal. The air pressure popped.

His mate bond lit up like a sunbeam. Finally!

A moment later, Chantal stepped through, wearing a uniform shirt and pants. She dropped her bag and launched straight at him.

He caught her in his arms and twirled, taking in her scent. Aiming a kiss at her mouth, he instead got her nose.

She laughed as she cupped his face in her hands. "I missed you." Fortunately, her kiss didn't miss.

Nibi's loud whistle distracted him. "Not to spoil the reunion or anything, but the sooner we finish this, the sooner we can get out of here." Her indulgent smile lessened the testiness of her complaint.

Dauro pulsed his love for Chantal through their connection, then set her down.

She wrapped her arm around his waist and snuggled under his shoulder. "You're right. I have news, and I want to hear yours."

Her welcome warmth made him realize the air was colder than he'd noticed. He didn't know if he'd changed or the demesne had changed. Or both.

Zephyr curled her little finger. The portal shut with an ear-popping snap.

A subtle tickle of magic came from Chantal as she looked around. "This place looks the same, but it feels amazingly better." She held up her hand as if feeling for rain. Tiny points of light appeared to dance over her palm. "The demesne seems happy."

Zephyr grinned. "Thank you for noticing. I'm still sorting out the quirks." Her eyes darted to Sunscar and back again. "It's a work in progress."

"Have you figured out yet how the demesne survived after Nessireth died?"

Zephyr blew out a loud breath. "No, other than it has something to do with how she fused her magic into the living rock and shaped the demesne around it."

Rosinette joined their circle, clutching the e-reader to her chest.

"I'll start," said Nibi. "After the underground auction house sold Kelvin to Nessireth, his aunt escaped during a big prison break. The Shifter Tribunal reunited them last week." She shaded her eyes and looked up at Dauro. "I know where they live."

Dauro didn't need Sunscar's telepathic network to know Nibi meant to visit them soon to check. He intended to be with her. The young shifter had been through much and deserved to be well cared for.

Rosinette looked up. "How are Yipkash and Rayapkhal?" The notes in her tone sang of missing them.

Dauro smiled. "They are the proud parents of seventeen." He grinned at his friends' astonishment.

Chantal gaped up at him. "Is that typical?"

"No. It's the largest birth in the last five centuries." He circled a finger upward. "Their healers think exposure to fairy demesne magic might have caused it."

Nibi raised an eyebrow. "I hope capricorns have nannies, or Yip and Raya will never sleep again."

"The whole clan is helping. It's their miracle." He squeezed Chantal's shoulders. "Wait until you see their land house. Five island cabins could fit inside."

"Are you going with him to Greece?" Rosinette tilted her head quizzically.

Chantal nodded. "After my final week in Barron, yes. Kotoyeesinay owes me twelve weeks of vacation, so I'm taking them all." She nudged Dauro with her hip. "My mate will need time to recover from my family and friends."

Dauro laughed. "I'm looking forward to meeting them."

"What about Trixis and Omorachi?" asked Chantal.

Nibi's smile turned feral. "They're in deep alligators. They are both fugitives from fairy justice, and their antics cost their tribe the demesne. If they'd have just let us go, we'd have all moved on, and the tribe could have claimed it with none the wiser." Nibi crossed her arms. "Hiring the auction house and the hunters demonstrated their intent. The Shifter Tribunal lawyers used Nessireth's book to prove she wasn't a tribe member when she died. The Celestial Fairy Court awarded the demesne to us six prisoners as compensation."

Dauro didn't know what to think about that. Everything he currently owned fit in one soft-sided bag. What would he do with a demesne?

The mate bond pulsed briefly with a soothing message from Chantal. *You don't have to decide today, love.*

She was right of course, which was another thing to thank the gods for.

Rosinette turned to Nibi. "What are your plans?"

"Find my sister. Find a lake to call my own." She cracked a sardonic smile. "Learn to use the internet."

"You might check out Fort LeBlanc, the sanctuary town in Canada." said Chantal. "They've organized 'welcome to the modern world' classes for some of the ahklut that stayed."

"Ahklut?" Nibi blinked. "As in the Terror of the North? They're back?"

"Yep. They're reformed. Well, mostly."

Sunscar stepped closer. "Has Kotoyeesinay read our proposal?"

"They have," replied Chantal. "They're interested. I have a draft agreement in my bag."

"Proposal?" It was the first Dauro had heard of it. And from the expressions of Nibi and Rosinette, the first they'd heard of it, too. He looked at his friend expectantly.

Sunscar's hair stilled. "This is why I asked you all to come back to the demesne together. First, to see how the demesne and statutes are not your enemies, and second, to discuss this." He tilted his chin toward Zephyr. "We proposed that the demesne become a refugee center for others like me who aren't ready for the real world. Who need a sheltered place for transition. We'd all have to agree of course, including Kelvin's aunt. And we'd need help from others to create habitats."

Dauro wished they still had the telepathic network to tell him how Sunscar felt about it. "Would you be the *sinchi*?" Dauro couldn't think of the English word.

"No, I am a bad leader. I terrify everyone. I will manage the castle and statues." Sunscar tilted his chin toward Zephyr again. "She will manage the demesne and help move the anchors to Kotoyeesinay when the time comes. We asked the town to help us find demesne specialists, therapists, and an appropriate director."

"Intriguing," said Nibi. "A halfway house for magic folk. You'll have a ton of details to sort, but if you're willing to do it, I'll sign off on the deal." A sharp smile passed her lips. "And just imagine how much it would have pissed off Nessireth to share with others."

Dauro snorted in amusement.

Rosinette squared her shoulders. "I will be your first resident."

Dauro didn't try to keep worry off his face. "You often talked about missing your family."

"I know, but..." Rosinette's shoulders tightened. "They won't have missed me."

The bleak, discordant music under her words made Dauro wince.

"If you'd like someone to talk to about it," said Chantal, "the *klenath* wyvern known as the Scholar of the Skies makes his home in Kotoyeesinay. I could introduce you."

Rosinette's eyes widened in surprise. She opened her mouth to speak, hesitated, then shook her head. "I will consider it. Thank you for the offer."

"You'd be welcome in Kotoyeesinay." She snapped her fingers, then dug into the bellows pocket on her thigh and brought out thin metal rectangles with small straps. "Speaking of which, these luggage tags are for each of you. They're guest tokens that will exempt you from the 'get-lost' spells in case you want to visit."

Sunscar held his up for a moment, then buckled the strap onto the chain he wore around his neck, next to a charm. Dauro couldn't resist teasing him. "You'd have a pocket for that if you'd wear pants."

Sunscar scowled imperiously. "Neither wraiths nor eels wear clothes."

Zephyr rolled her eyes. "Like I said, work in progress."

Nibi looked at the new watch on her wrist. "Since Chantal still has to do time in Florida, how about Dauro and I go see Kelvin and his aunt about the demesne proposal?"

Chantal laughed. "You make it sound like I'm working off a jail sentence."

Nibi snorted. "All the land cougars I knew were kitty-brained. If that dopey male you told me about is anything to go by, they haven't changed."

"You mean Fontaine? He won't be bothering anyone for a while."

"Did you transform him into a slug?" asked Rosinette hopefully.

Chantal laughed. "No, but I appreciate your confidence in my ability." She hooked a thumb over her belt. "My first day back, I fixed the noisy air vent above my desk and discovered a wireless surveillance camera. Three others, too. When the sheriff threatened to bring in a wizard with a truth geas spell, Fontaine confessed. He thought I was hooking up with the other deputies. The proof was supposed to get us all fired. Instead, the sheriff busted him to probationary foot patrol for the next year."

Dauro had already heard some of the story. Fontaine had first tried to claim that Chantal had done it. Although he'd been away from his mate for too many days already, perhaps it would be better to go with Nibi. If he went to Barron, he might be tempted to introduce himself to the cougar who had tried to shove Chantal off the bus.

Their mental connection strengthened as Chantal tightened her arm around his waist. *Thank you, love, but the sheriff took away his gun privileges, too. That'll humiliate Fontaine far worse than being sat on by a prehistoric sloth.*

Dauro caught Nibi's eye. "I would like to go with you to visit Kelvin." He frowned. "But I have nothing to trade for portal passage."

"We've got a year's worth of free trips coming from the Celestial Court as part of our compensation." Nibi pointed to the box on the bench behind her. "Besides, Rosinette told me which of Nessireth's charms and wands are safe to sell, and your clever mate knows a dark elf in Kotoyeesinay who can help us get top price. Even split six ways, you'll have plenty of money."

His new memories said money was like a future promise to trade, but he didn't understand how it worked. From something Chantal had said, he gathered she had money held in trust, so maybe she could explain it to him. So much to learn about the real world.

So many important decisions to make, too, but not right then. The gods had truly blessed him with a mate who understood his need for time to think.

"Then let's go see Kelvin." He turned and stepped closer to Sunscar. "I owe you more than I can say for teaching me, for being my friend. For helping me make friends with the others." He held up his wrist with the demesne-to-world charm Chantal had made for them. "If you ever need help, or just someone to talk to, call me. I'll be calling you, too."

Sunscar nodded gravely. "I will answer." He hesitantly reached out to pat Dauro's upper arm. "You saved me, too. You taught me hope."

Dauro opened his arms, but let Sunscar step into them before giving his friend a tight, hard hug.

To Dauro's surprise, Sunscar then turned to Nibi and hugged her, whispering something in her ear.

Nibi nodded and responded in a language Dauro didn't know.

Zephyr whistled. "I know you all think fairies are impatient, but we've got nothing on flamingos. They're pinging at the guest portal."

Chantal laughed. "They're probably worried about you. They're still convinced my starving leopard wants to eat everyone."

"We're done here, anyway. Let's not keep them waiting." With a rush of fairy magic from Zephyr's careless gesture, the portal opened with a quick glow and a pop of air pressure. Dauro couldn't imagine what it would be like to have so much power at his fingertips.

A blast of heat and a blaze of sunshine poured into the demesne from the portal. Their flamingo escorts stood warily well back on the Vieques mountaintop.

Sunscar moved to the side of the portal entrance where he couldn't be seen. "Safe travels."

Nibi grabbed her box, one-arm hugged Rosinette, and strode through the portal. Chantal picked up her bag and handed it to Zephyr. "I brought some things to tide you over until your next real-world visit."

Zephyr's eyebrows rose. "What did you bring?"

Chantal laughed. "You'll have to open it and see." She held out her hand to Dauro, who was happy to take it.

He waved to Rosinette and nodded to Sunscar, then stepped through the portal with the shifter he loved and who loved him back. He could handle whatever the real world dealt him, as long as he had friends and his mate beside him.

Chantal laughed and squeezed his hand. *You think the sweetest things.*

~ ~ ~

Thank you for reading **Shifter's Storm**. I hope you loved how Chantal and Dauro navigated their unorthodox courtship while rescuing their friends and themselves.

More books are coming soon. In the meantime, if you don't want your trip to the Ice Age Shifters world to end, you could go back in time to **Shifter Mate Magic** (Ice Age Shifters #1) to read how Chantal's mother Jackie met Trevor. He's a lonely prehistoric bear shifter. She's running for her life and doesn't have time for romance.

Do you like to post reviews of books? I'd appreciate an honest review at your favorite booksellers and/or Goodreads. They really help other readers find good stories to read.

If you like paranormal romance, check out **In Graves Below** in the shared worlds of S.E. Smith's Magic, New Mexico series.

And if you love futuristic romance, check out my space opera, action, and romance series that starts with **Last Ship Off Polaris-G** and **Overload Flux**. There's a big damn story arc going on about evolution and rebellion.

Don't miss out on finding out about upcoming releases, author appearances. Sign up for my monthly newsletter at https://bit.ly/CVN--news.